KARMA'S KISS 2

A NOVEL BY

SNOOK

Amarquis Publications, LLC
P.O. Box 34224
North Chesterfield, VA 23234

Library of Congress Control Number: 2015946175

ISBN: 978-0-692-77773-2

First Amarquis Publications Paperback Edition September 2016

Printed in the United States

Cover art & interior designed by Indie Designz

Model: Kandace J. Minor-Ross
sminorross@gmail.com

ALSO BY SNOOK

KARMA'S KISS

THE DOWN TURN

ISSUES OF THE HEART

THE DAY THE WALLS CRIED

ACKNOWLEDGEMENTS

I thank God for blessing me through this writing journey. Thank you for the words to bring this book to completion. I have to first apologize for the long wait for this book. This didn't come easy. Writing part two was harder than I expected. The pressure to continue the same momentum was real.

Karma's Kiss is my first baby. This book will always be my first love. To continue this story and bring it to an end was bittersweet. I hope that you enjoy the story as much as I enjoyed creating it. Thank you for all of those that stayed on me asking when part two was coming out and for all of the encouragement. That kept me writing. Thank you for waiting so patiently for me to craft this book.

To my day one readers, I will never forget you and your support when Karma's Kiss was first published. It was a rough start, but you hung in there with me and I will never forget that. Here it is what you all have been waiting for. Enjoy!

Much love,

Snook

This book is dedicated to all of my supporters.

CHAPTER 1

Marlon

I stared at the handwritten letter in my hand. I read each word for the second time but this time more carefully. It was written in Suga's handwriting. The swirly letters, perfect spacing, and the signature was authentic. Yet, I couldn't believe the words that were written on the paper before me. There was no way she left me; no way would she leave our son. There was no way she did the things that she was being accused of.

Where is my son?

I reached into my pants pocket and pulled out my cell phone. Normally, my mother would call to let me know every update concerning Marlon Jr. She would call to tell me how well he was taking his bottle, when he went down for a nap and when he awoke from his naps. She was a wonderfully involved grandmother and I loved her for that.

I frantically dialed my mother's phone number, doubting

with each second that Marlon Jr. was with her. As the phone rang, I read over the note to be sure that it said what I thought it was saying. Each ring felt like it was taking time from my life and the life of my son. On the fourth ring, I headed out of the kitchen and to the garage, running my hands through my hair; something I often did when I was under pressure. Finally, I heard my mother's soft voice.

"Hi, Marlon," my mother said. Her sweet, calm tone almost relaxed me.

"Mom, is Marlon Jr. with you? Please tell me you have my son!" I said anxiously. I felt my knees buckle under me as I waited for her response.

"Yes, he's here. Suga dropped him off a couple of hours ago. She told me not to bother you because she had something special planned for the two of you this evening. Is there something wrong, son?"

She had something special planned all right.

"Thank you, Jesus! He's fine, right?"

"Yes, Junior is fine. What's going on?"

"Mom, I need you to keep him with you. I promise I'll talk to you about it when I get there."

"That's fine son. I'd already planned to keep him for the night. You know that I don't mind watching my baby. You and Suga take all the time you need. Junior is just fine."

Just then, I heard Marlon Jr. babbling in the background and that put a smile on my face knowing that my son was definitely out of harm's way. My heart was somewhat at ease.

"Mom, don't let Junior leave without me. Even if Suga comes, don't let her take him. Call me, all right?"

"Sure Marlon," she said hesitantly.

After hanging up with my mother I went to my office. The house was too quiet. It felt empty as if no one lived there. I focused on Suga since I knew that my son was safe. I couldn't see how she could up and leave just when things were getting back to normal. We were getting our marriage back on track. Kendra was no longer an issue or her daughter, Destiny. It was sad that things played out the way that they did.

If what the detective said about Suga was true, then I understood. But there was no way Suga could kill anyone and then set me up for the murders. I know I heard her voice leave the message with the detectives that implicated me, but I refused to believe that she would do that to me. If she killed L.C. and her girlfriend, I could understand her fleeing from fear of going to prison. My heart would not allow me to believe it. Suga was possibly a fugitive of the law. The other possibility was that she would be returning home soon. Our family would be intact and all of the accusations against us would be proven to be untrue. I needed to clear my mind and decide what the next step should be.

I found my office in shambles. Someone had pulled out the contents of my desk. Papers and folders were all over the desk and floor. The bookshelf was missing books that were strewed all over the floor. It was strange to find this one room ransacked. The rest of the house or at least downstairs was just the way Suga kept it, immaculate.

I rushed over to my desk to find the set of books I kept for the jewelry store. The hidden compartment of the desk was still intact although the drawer was pulled out and sitting on the floor. The money that was in the desk was missing along with the business checkbooks. The desk lamp was knocked over and laying on a stack of crumpled papers.

"Shit! Suga!" I shouted.

Things were looking more like a robbery. Realizing that I didn't do a thorough check of the house for Suga, I bolted towards the stairs calling out to her.

"Suga! Answer me! Where are you?"

It was no longer looking as if she left on her own accord. The letter and the condition of the house didn't add up. Once I reached the master bedroom, I knew. It looked like a struggle took place. Her clothes were pulled out of the drawers. The items that were lined on her dresser were knocked to the floor. Perfume bottles were broken, leaving a strong smell in the room. Her closet was the same except the missing suitcase that was always on the top shelf. The sheets from the bed were pulled away and hanging to the floor. I tried Suga's phone again as I searched the other bedrooms, bathrooms and closets. She was nowhere to be found. I knew then that she was taken.

Someone was after me and my family and I didn't know who. I needed someone to help me make sense of it all so I decided to call Dee. Dee had become distant, but he was still my right hand man. Losing Kendra changed him. I tried to give him his space to grieve and find his place. Dee's phone went straight to voicemail. I contemplated leaving a message, but decided against it.

My last choice was phoning the police. I reached in my

pocket for the detective's business card. They were the ones who wanted Suga for murder. I wasn't sure if they were really going to have her best interest at heart if I was to tell them she was abducted. There wasn't any more time to waste, so I decided to report her missing. I began to dial the phone number on the card. Before pressing the send button, I received a call from Dee on my cell phone.

"What's up, man," I said.

"Playing with Destiny. What's up," Dee said.

"I have a situation over at the house. I need you to get over here."

"What the fuck is your problem? I just told you I was playing with my daughter."

"I understand you are spending time with your daughter, but this is an emergency! I really need you to get over here."

"What the fuck I look like? Every time your ass have a problem, I solve it!"

"Every time your ass need a bailout, I do it! Don't come at me with that bullshit. You know what it is!"

I could feel the veins in my neck bulging as I screamed into the phone.

Dee laughed on the other end of the phone. He sounded crazy.

"What the fuck is funny?" I asked.

"Always needing me to put in work. That's what you keep me around for, right? We used to be best friends… Naw, fuck that. We were brothers. Neither one of us was bigger than the other one. When I ate, you ate. We used to eat together. Now I've been reduced to table scraps while you eat like a king! You call me to clean up your mess."

"I don't know what the hell your problem is, but I have bigger problems than your ass! You've been on some other shit lately, but I've been giving your ass a pass because of Kendra's death. You had the same opportunities I had. You could've invested your money like I did. When are you going to man up and stop blaming other people for your problems? My doors have always been open. You always did what you wanted to do."

"Everybody don't want to be like you; a sellout."

There was a pause.

I said, "I see how you really feel."

I ended the call with Dee. I didn't have time for his antics and jealous rage. He must've been drinking or high to talk to me like that. This was not the first time that we'd had this very same fight. It just seemed to happen more often.

My cell phone rang again. It was Dee calling back. I started not to answer, but I needed his help in spite of our differences.

"What's up, man?" I asked.

"My bad, man. I didn't mean to come off like that. Look, just forget about it. You know I've been going through some shit. It's rough raising my daughter on my own. It's been tough since Kendra been gone. I've been trying to hold all of this down on my own. I look at your family and I see where I fucked up. You were right, I had the opportunity to go into business, but I blew my money on bullshit."

"It ain't even about that. You've been coming at me like a hating ass bitch. I ain't never seen you out here cold, so don't bite the hand that feeds you, feel me. Anything you need, you know I got you and Destiny."

"Yeah, you're right. My bad. I'll see you as soon as I can."

"I'm at the house."

"I got you."

There was an uncomfortable silence. I didn't know what to say and Dee was showing how he really felt. He was jealous. I'm sure he was always jealous, but he was just growing the balls to show it.

Dee hung up before I could say anything else. Since Kendra died, he wasn't the same, especially towards me. He'd been more distant and cold. With Suga missing, and now Dee being unreliable, I didn't know where to turn. I could've called Gooch, but he would need a target, but I didn't know who or what the target was.

CHAPTER 2

Linwood

The past month was rough on the inside. One visit from Redd informing me that Trey killed the love of my life, Teesa and tried to kill Suga, set me back. I relived the first time that I found out that Teesa was dead, only this time, she really was. He told me that Teesa died protecting our daughter from Trey. Nothing prepared me for the news, especially about Trey. He had the nerve to come for my money after all these years. Come to find out, he did a little bid and came out hungry. He almost killed my daughter and put my grandson's life in jeopardy. I knew I did my shit in the streets, but I didn't hurt anyone to get my paper. Everyone I robbed wanted to be robbed. No one ever was hurt. All they had to do was defraud the insurance companies and we all got paid.

I worried about Suga night and day. After her visit, things seemed so final between us. She didn't seem open to rebuilding our relationship or my love. I thought it best to let her heal and get back to some sort of normalcy before reaching out to her. Every day I walked around with a heavy heart, but tried to show strength on my exterior. The only thing that kept me sane was knowing that I was possibly going to be released early.

I walked briskly back to my cell. I looked at Lamar and gave a nod. Lamar walked out, stood in front of our cell door, and leaned over the balcony to be a look out. There were the usual ramblings down below.

I glanced over my shoulder before removing a small cell phone from under Lamar's thin mattress. I turned the small cell phone over in my hand as I searched for the power button. As I waited for the phone to come on, I looked out. Lamar gave a nod letting me know that it was clear. I waited for the home screen to appear. Once on, I dialed a phone number.

"Hello?" a deep voice answered.

"It's me, Linwood. Tell me you have good news for me."

"It's done. We're just waiting for the judge to review the paperwork and sign for your release," Kyle said.

Kyle was one of Richmond's top criminal defense attorneys. From murder cases to high profile drug cases, he was the man. If he didn't get his clients off, he would cut some of the sweetest deals that a man could have in his situation. My deal was abandoned when the judge, that was once a client of mine, wanted to be as far away from the case as he could. The case was passed on to another judge that was known for being a hammer. This was one time my influence and Kyle couldn't make the deal.

"I don't trust these judges. That fat fuck screwed me! He was the main one I scored for. As soon as shit hit the fan, he tucked his ass and ran. This judge better not fuck me this time."

"I made sure I reminded him of that. Look, it took many years and favors to get where we are today. You have a lot to be thankful for," Kyle said.

"How long is this going to take?" I asked.

"Anywhere from thirty to sixty days. Hang in there. You're almost home. I've done my part as your attorney and we need this judge to do his," Kyle said.

"Thirty to sixty days? I want out like yesterday. If it takes any longer, I might as well serve the few years I have left!" I yelled into the phone.

There was a brief silence.

"More money can speed up things. Honestly, he's asking for more money than you have right now. I might can get him down. Just know that if I do this, you could be coming home to nothing," Kyle explained. "Do you have another way of getting this money? I'll hate for you to come home to nothing."

"How much money do I have left? I know that I had more than enough to take care of this. You better not be fucking with my money!" I yelled into the phone. I quickly lowered my tone and looked over my shoulder. He was starting to piss me off.

"Your account has dwindled tremendously with my legal fees, payoffs, and you know that other thing we had to take care of," Kyle said.

"I have money but…" I stopped talking.

I thought about Suga, the key to the rest of my paper and my home. I'd given Suga the key to my fortune, well, what was left of it. I had money stashed in my attic and a safe deposit box with three hundred thousand dollars. Thanks to the bank manager being one of my clients, I was able to put the safe deposit box in Suga's name. No one knew about this but Teesa.

"Do you have a way to pay him for that signature and still be able to take care of yourself when you get home? I have to advise you that it won't be smart to come home to nothing. That can land you right back inside. I've seen this happen before," Kyle asked.

"No, I'm tapped out. Pay him everything I have left. Just get me out of here. I have to go," I said.

"Okay, if that's what you want to do. Talk to you soon," Kyle said.

I quickly ended the call because I needed to place another one.

Lamar entered our cell with Skinny behind him. Skinny was in for his drug use. He would steal and rob to support his habit. Skinny was well known on the inside and outside. He was the son of a congressman. At one time, Skinny was a college boy with high aspirations to follow in his father's footsteps. Things went wrong for Skinny after his mother's death. She died unexpectedly from a brain aneurysm. After her funeral, he never returned to college. He turned to drugs to deal with her death.

"What is it?" I asked impatiently.

"He's out here about to cause a scene. I told him to come back later," Lamar said.

Lamar stared Skinny down. Skinny looked over to me with a cocky smirk on his face.

"It's cool. Give us a minute," I told Lamar.

Lamar left the cell without any questions. He eyed Skinny up and down before leaving, sending him a clear message that he would deal with him later.

"Do we still have a deal?" Skinny asked.

"If you were able to get that information I asked you for," I said.

"A three month supply, right? No shorts?" Skinny asked. Skinny began to scratch a dark, dry patch of skin on his arm.

"Three months of your drug of choice and we know what that is," I said.

Skinny looked around as if someone else was in the cell with us before he spoke.

"I was able to find out what really happened with the judge and your lawyer. Check this out, the judge was never paid. That dirty ass lawyer of yours took your money. Word is he was the reason the fat fuck died of so called natural causes. He didn't want to leave no witnesses behind. You were right, his ass is as dirty as they come. For some reason he didn't want you to come home," Skinny said.

"After all these years I've been wasting away in here because I was robbed by my own lawyer. Story of my fucking life," I said.

"Do you have a little something for me now?" Skinny asked.

"Yeah, see Lamar. He'll take care of you," I said.

I was finally able to get the truth. I paid him to keep me out of prison. Money wasn't a problem if there was a price I could pay. Now he was stalling my release. Something was up and I needed to find out fast.

I needed to speak to Suga. She had the key to my life after this shit hole. I didn't want to press her so soon after coming home from the hospital after being attacked by Trey. If I could dig up his body, I'd kill his ass all over again. He violated me by going after my flesh and blood; my daughter. Worst of all, he killed her mother, the only woman I'd ever loved. As soon as my feet hit the pavement, I was going to piss and shit on his grave.

CHAPTER 3

Dee

I turned the bottle of beer up to my mouth taking in large gulps. I used the back of my hand to wipe the beer that dripped down the sides of my mouth. Destiny sat Indian style on the floor watching cartoons while playing with her dolls.

What would he do without me? He calls me to handle all his dirt. What has he done for me?

I seethed with hatred for Marlon. His call for help infuriated me. I poured out the rest of my beer because I no longer had a taste for it. Marlon just didn't know how much I hated him for treating me like his flunky. I was no one's flunky. I was my own man. I was a boss. It was becoming harder and harder to stomach him, his perfect wife, and their perfect life. I was all alone with my daughter now. After the death of my wife, Kendra, my life hasn't been the same. Destiny constantly asks about her mother. She's too young to understand that her mother was shot and killed in the very home we sleep in every night. She would never understand that I too was a target, but I somehow survived. I cursed God for taking Kendra away, but I was thankful that my daughter wasn't harmed. I can't help but think how things could've played out. I live with guilt every day. If I could've traded my life for hers I would've.

I still fought the memory of Kendra riding Marlon's dick. When I walked in on the two of them, I should've murdered them both. If it weren't for Kendra carrying my seed, I would've murdered them both. But no, her conniving ass came up with a brilliant scheme that kept us in his pockets for a while. Then I fucked his precious wife, Suga, in return for his generosity. Suga sure was sweet.

I find myself blaming both Marlon and Suga for my family's demise. Suga made Kendra feel like she wasn't good enough. She always showed Kendra up. Marlon made me look bad by outdoing everything I wanted to do for Kendra. When Kendra and I purchased our home, Marlon went out and purchased a bigger house. When I bought my Benz, he went out and bought the newer model with all the upgrades. After the death of Kendra and the failed attempt on my life, I lost it. The only thing that kept me sane at times was my daughter. The other times when she wasn't around, I had no control.

Now a single father, life was harder than ever. With the help of my sister, Chrissy, Destiny was able to have some normality. She spent most of her time with her aunt and cousins. When she wasn't with Chrissy, my mother had her.

A knock on the door snapped me back to reality. Destiny ran to the front door first.

"Hold on, baby girl. Let daddy get that," I said, running behind her.

I reached the door just as Destiny placed her hand on the handle. I placed my hand on hers. Destiny looked up at me with the most beautiful smile. She looked just like her mother. Time froze as I thought about Kendra. I missed her. Destiny reminded me of her so much. Maybe that was the reason I limited my time with her. The more time I spent with my daughter, the more I thought about Kendra.

I opened the door to find my sister, Chrissy, and my niece, Deandra.

"Hey, brother! I was on this side of town. So I decided to come on by and get Destiny," Chrissy said.

"Hey, sis. Come on in," I said.

I closed the door behind them, but not before scanning my surroundings. I was always paranoid not knowing when or if the killer would return to finish the job. I didn't see anyone other than the neighbors loading up their minivan with their three children and two dogs.

"Hi, Uncle Dee," Deandra said. She reached up for a hug.

"Hi, princess," I said. I lifted her up in my arms.

Destiny tugged on her cousin's feet and said, "My daddy!"

"No need to fight girls," I said.

I picked Destiny up too. I hugged them both tightly and quickly put them down. My shoulder ached with pain where I was shot. I rubbed my shoulder and the girls ran off.

"How have you been feeling? Is your shoulder still bothering you?" Chrissy asked.

"Yeah, from time to time," I said.

"I told you to finish physical therapy. If you would've listened, your shoulder wouldn't be bothering you so much. You're so hard headed. Some things never change," she said.

"You're right. I've been thinking about going back. Those muscle relaxers they…" I started.

"Did you hear something?" she asked.

"Hear what?" I asked.

We both paused. The girls ran back into the living room with Destiny's overnight bag a teddy bear. She never left the house without her bear.

"What's wrong daddy? Is it those rats again?" Destiny asked.

"What rats?" Chrissy asked.

"We have rats in the basement. The exterminator will be out in a couple of days," I said.

I quickly moved them along. After kissing my daughter goodbye, I felt relieved. I watched as Chrissy and the girls drove off.

I had business to handle. I had to be captain save a hoe once again for Marlon. He couldn't bust a grape without me busting one first. What would he do without me? I put in all of the work. He just gives the orders. One day soon, I'll have him at my mercy.

Marlon

decided to backtrack to the garage to see if there were any signs of a struggle. It seemed to be undisturbed in comparison to the rest of the house. I looked around to see if anything was out of place. Everything seemed as it was. I walked across the concrete floor towards the metal shelving I had installed to store my power tools. There, I did notice something. The two tubs that Suga took from her parent's house were placed under old newspapers and other junk as if she was trying to hide them.

Reaching on the top shelf, my hands searched for a box. I pulled down a gray metal lock box. My curiosity pulled at me. Something was telling me to open the tubs. I removed my keys from my pocket and unlocked the box. Inside was a Chief Special .45. I rubbed a thumb across the name and logo engraved on the barrel. Although compact, this pistol was flawless with a six shot magazine. I'd kept it out in the garage, because Suga didn't want guns inside of our home. Out of respect for her, I gladly stored my baby in the garage. Big Brother was inside the house on the top shelf of my closet. I kept the shotgun in a duffel bag. Suga was unaware.

I looked at the tubs. I didn't want to invade her privacy, especially after everything that she'd been through. I slid the two tubs out into the middle of the floor. One of them was much lighter than I remembered. I opened the lighter tub first. There were family photos and a quilt. I shifted through the photos. This tub was much heavier when I lifted it into the back of my trunk. Whatever contents inside were now gone. I slid the tub back.

I opened the second tub. The air left my lungs as I stared down at bundles of cash money. I picked up a bundle. There were nothing but one hundred dollar bills bundled together. I picked up another and then another, finding the same thing.

"Where the fuck did this come from?" I said.

Shit just wasn't making sense. I saw her haul both of the tubs out of her parent's house. She never once said she found any money. This once again confirmed my suspicions that Suga didn't leave on her own. She would've taken that money with her, no doubt about that.

"Fuck!" I shouted.

I placed the money back into the tub and placed it where I found it. I tucked my gun in my waist and headed inside.

The doorbell was ringing. I quickly rushed to the front door. I looked out of the window. I didn't see any other vehicles.

I stood behind the door and called out, "Who is it?"

I waited for a response. There wasn't one.

"Who the fuck is it? Speak the fuck up or die where you stand?" I shouted through the door. I pointed my gun and aimed at the door.

"It's me, Santé," a female voice said from the other side of the door.

"Santé?" I repeated.

"Yes, it's me, cousin. Open the damn door," she said.

I lowered my gun, but I didn't put it away. I slowly opened the door and standing on my doorstep was the image of Suga. Santé, was Suga's twin, although they were cousins. They looked so much alike that I broke down at the sight of her.

"What's wrong with you?" Santé asked. She rushed in and caught me as I was falling to the floor. I wanted so much for her to be Suga. She was supposed to be safe at home.

"They took her," I managed to say.

"They who? Who took who?" Santé asked.

"Suga is gone. Somebody took her."

"Are you sure? I spoke to her yesterday and everything seemed fine."

"The police came to the store today asking questions about Suga. They said she was involved in the murder of her friend L.C. and her girlfriend. When I got home, I found a letter from her saying she was leaving me. But I found a stash of money I know she wouldn't have left behind."

"Yeah, I know she wouldn't have left money behind not unless she planned on coming back for it."

I looked at her suspiciously. Her eyes darted around and she began to stutter. She knew she said the wrong thing.

"What do you know about that shit in my garage?" I asked.

I yanked away from her. Santé had guilt written all over her pretty, little face.

"Let me get my bags and we can talk about this. If something happened to my cousin, I don't know what I would do. We don't have any time to waste," Santé said.

She rushed back out of the house. I went into the living room to wait. Santé returned with two suitcases.

"What is all of that?" I asked.

"Oh, Suga said I can stay for a week or so while I'm visiting but I'm early. I wasn't supposed to come until tomorrow," she said. "I guess I wasn't early enough."

I took a deep breath and shook my head.

"Is that going to be a problem?" Santé asked.

"No, you're family. You know you're always welcome here."

Santé sat across from me. It was hard to look at her. The resemblance was too much for me to stand.

"What are we going to do?" she asked.

"Why are you so damn calm about this shit?"

"Look at you? You're damn near falling apart. One of us has to hold it together for Suga. Besides, I think better when I'm calm."

"Do you think it's somebody from Linwood's past again? There could be more people like Trey out there."

"I seriously doubt it. After all these years, I was shocked that Trey came as hard as he did. I don't know what made him think that there was still money left after my uncle was locked up," she said. "Right now, we need to focus on finding Suga. Where is Junior?"

"He's fine. He's with my mother," I said.

We both sat in silence. My cell phone rang.

"Hello?" I asked.

"Be there in five," Dee said.

"Cool," I said hanging up.

I felt some relief that Dee was on the way. I didn't really trust him, but I needed his help.

"Who was that?" Santé asked.

"My boy, Dee. I need him right now. That's my right hand man," I said. I stood to my feet. "Go ahead upstairs and get settled in while we talk."

I picked up Santé's suitcases and followed her upstairs to the guest room. It was hard to ignore her body. She wore leggings with a cut off shirt, exposing her stomach and back. With every step, her ass bounced. My eyes were glued to her.

When she reached the top of the stairs, she stopped and turned to look at me. It was too late; she caught me eyeing her ass. The look on her face let me know that she would castrate me if she thought I was thinking something inappropriate.

"You can take the guest room down the hall on the right. If you need fresh linen, they are in the closet. Make yourself at home," I said.

I stood there with suitcases in both hands with pie on my face.

"I can take it from here, thank you," Santé said.

I handed her the suitcases and headed back downstairs. I shook off the awkward feeling of having Santé in the house without Suga being here. I went back into the office and began to pick up the books and papers that were on the floor. My mind raced thinking about where Suga could be and who was responsible.

CHAPTER 5

Santé

I walked past Suga and Marlon's room. The door was slightly open. I've never seen her room look out of place or anything out of place in that house, something definitely happened. I'd held my emotions together while talking to Marlon because I've never trusted him. Suga loved him, but she'd told me about the affair and possible child he had with her best friend Kendra. For all I know, he could've done something to her. The last time I saw Suga, she wanted me to get rid of a few things for her. She might've been trying to leave him and needed the money.

I walked down the hall to the guest room. I opened the door and found it to be just as immaculate as the rest of the house. It had Suga written all over it. I closed the door behind me and the suitcases fell from my hands as I tried to mask my cry with my hands. The nervous energy that I contained in Marlon's presence slowly left my body. I couldn't believe what he told me. I couldn't believe that Suga was taken. If she was taken, Marlon probably had something to do with it.

"Oh my, God!" I cried. "God, please let Suga be okay. Wherever she is Lord, please keep her safe."

I had a good ugly cry with smeared makeup and a runny nose. I pulled out my phone and dialed Suga's number. It went straight to voicemail. I tried her three more times, leaving a message the third time.

I pulled myself together. I knew I had to talk to my Uncle Linwood to let him know what was going on. I also had to call Ali. If I was right about Marlon having something to do with Suga's disappearance, I was going to need him.

I sat on the bed and called my boyfriend, Ali.

"Hey, baby," I said.

"Hey. Are you there already? I didn't expect you to call for another hour or so."

"I just got here. Listen, I arrived to some bad news about my cousin."

My voice was shaky as I tried not to have another crying fit.

"Why are you talking like that? You good?" Ali asked.

"No, I'm not! Suga is missing. Her husband said that somebody took her, but tried to make it look like she left him or something. I'm not sure what's going on," I said.

"What the fuck? Suga is missing?" Ali asked.

"Yes, baby. She's not here. She's not answering her phone. It looks like there was a struggle in her bedroom. It's all fucked up and I know that isn't her. I think Marlon had something to do with it, but I'm not sure. I have to do some investigating," I said. I took a brief pause. "We're not going to be able to go along with the plans," I whispered.

"Calm down, Santé. There's nothing to keep us from going along with our plans. Suga is probably somewhere mad and spending his money," he said.

"You're wrong. Something isn't right. She knew I was coming with this money. She would've been here, trust me."

"She's going to turn up. Nothing is going to change. The plans are already in motion and there's no turning back now."

I kicked myself.

"Did he call the police?" Ali asked.

"Exactly! No damn police were here when I got here. He has a friend that is on the way over. Baby, I need you. If he did have something to do with it, I don't want to be here alone with him," I said.

"Fuck that. You can stay at a hotel. You don't have to stay there with him! Shit changed. I know you wanted to spend time with your people, but she ain't there now."

"I know that. Maybe I should stay here so that I can figure out what's really going on. As soon as I find out what happened to my cousin then I'll leave."

"Look, don't make me come down there and burn down your city. I'm going to get my money and I'm not going to let anything get in the way of that."

"How can you think about that at a time like this? Suga is missing. I can't do that to her right now."

"This is a blessing in disguise. I feel for you and your cousin and I'm going to truly do everything in my power to help you find her. But I'm going to stick to our plan too. No one is going to get hurt and your cousin is going to be good."

"No, this is not the time for this. I didn't know all of this was going to happen. How could I have guessed that I was running into this tornado? No, we are not going to do this to her. You have to come up with another plan."

"I have a plan and I'm going to go through with it, thanks to you. Trust me baby, it will be all right. No one will ever know that we had anything to do with it."

"I don't know about this. You know what… I don't want to talk about this. I just want to find Suga."

"Okay, I'll let it go for now. I know how much she means to you. I'll try to get to you soon and see how I can help."

"Thanks, baby. I knew I could count on you," I said.

"You play him close if you don't trust him. If you need anything, call me. In the meantime, I'm sending Queenie down there," he said.

"Queenie? Don't send Queenie's crazy ass down here! She would cut Marlon's throat before I find out anything."

"It's already done. Queenie is on the way. I'll make sure she keep it calm. Call her if you need anything."

"Okay. Thank you, baby. I love you."

"I love you, too," he said.

I hung up the phone. He sure did put a smile on my face. I love that man. I knew Ali had my back in this. Ali was a boss. I'd never met a man quite like him. We first met three years ago while I was visiting a friend in New York. Ali came over with her boyfriend. I was attracted to his dark skin and tattoos. We talked all night and exchanged phone numbers.

Although he lived in New York and I lived in Virginia, we made our long distance relationship work.

After a year of traveling back and forth, he asked me to move to New York. I didn't know his lifestyle until I was permanently in New York. He was a thief. He robbed anyone for anything that he could score big. That included banks, businesses, and drug dealers. He gave me a choice, if I didn't like what he did for a living then I could walk. If I loved him like I said I did, then he wanted me to be a part of that life. I accepted him and his lifestyle. He had three people that were a part of his hustle that he considered family; Queenie, Raheem, and Dirt.

I was still uneasy about his determination to move forward with his plans. There was too much going on for me to worry about that. I had to deal with one problem at a time. I began to get settled in. I knew that as long as I had Ali on my side, Suga was going to come home. I also knew that if Suga was harmed in any way, he was going to see to it that somebody paid for it.

One thing was for sure, Marlon and I were going to have a sit down. It just didn't make any sense to me. I'd unloaded a lot of merchandise for Suga. One of my suitcases was full of fresh cash for her, minus my cut. There was cash in the wind and I know Suga wanted it. She was planning something, but I didn't think this was it.

I ran myself a hot bubble bath. As the tub filled with hot water, steam filled the room. I really needed to relax, gather my thoughts, and come up with a plan. As I began to undress, I got a strange feeling I was being watched. I knew no one else was in the room because the door was closed. Knowing that Marlon and I were alone in the house without Suga made it seem wrong. She would have never allowed that to happen; not that she didn't trust me. She just didn't trust the situation.

I ran to lock the door, but before I did, I peeked out into the hallway. I listened for Marlon and he was still downstairs. It sounded like he was talking to someone. My concerns for Suga were heightened when I saw something from the corner of my eye. Outside of her bedroom door, I saw her cane. The same one that I saw her with when she came home from the hospital. I didn't notice it at first. I knew that she needed her cane to walk. Her hip wasn't close to being healed to the point where she could walk without it. I quickly closed and locked the door.

I walked to my suitcase and removed a small bag. Inside was my 9mm. I cocked it and put one in the head. I took the gun with me to the bathroom for easier access, just in case things weren't what they seemed.

CHAPTER 6

Dee

I pulled up to the Cole's estate as Marlon liked to refer to it. We were supposed to be partners, but he seemed to benefit more from this partnership than I ever had. I loved him like a brother, but I hated him more. He always made me feel less than him.

Marlon was waiting at the front door when I pulled up. He was pacing back and forth. He looked both nervous and scared.

Getting out the car I said, "What's up, man?"

"Suga is gone!" Marlon said.

"What the fuck you're talking about she's gone? She probably out shopping or something? You know how she is."

"Dee, she's gone! I found a letter she wrote. It was on some Dear John shit! Our bedroom is all fucked up and she is nowhere to be found!"

"Wait a minute. A fucking Dear John letter? What the fuck did you do this time?"

"I ain't do shit. Things have been going great since she's been home from the hospital. One thing I know is that she didn't write that letter on her own. This is looking more like an abduction."

"So, you're telling me Suga left your ass?"

"Did you hear me? I think somebody took her! Come inside and tell me what you think about this. This shit don't make no sense."

I followed Marlon into the house.

Marlon walked over to the kitchen table and picked up a sheet of paper.

"When I came home this is what I found."

Marlon handed me a handwritten letter from Suga. I read the letter and handed it back to him.

"It says she left your ass," I said.

"Do you believe that shit? Because I don't," Marlon said. "Something ain't right, man. The police saying she killed L.C. and her bitch..."

"Hold up. They saying what? Where the fuck they get that from?"

"Did you handle that shit the way I told you? I told you to give her the money to leave town and never show her face in Virginia again. You didn't have them bitches killed did you?"

"I know you ain't questioning me about that shit now? I did what you told me to do. I paid that bitch and told her to leave. She took the money and said she needed a change of scenery anyway. That was the last time I saw her," I said.

"It's crazy how she was killed right after that, right?"

"Look, man. I don't know what you're getting at with that shit. But I ain't the enemy. I don't know why you're listening to them snakes anyway. Anybody could've killed them. All I know is that I didn't have anything to do with that."

"Too much shit is going on. I don't know what to think. All I know is that I have to find her."

"I agree. Look, let me hit the streets and see what the word is. You sit tight until I call you. Don't make any moves without me. We're going to find her. I got you, bro," I said.

"Thanks," Marlon said.

Marlon stepped back from me when I offered him my hand.

"What's the problem?" I asked.

"For a minute there you were tripping on me," he said.

"Fuck all that. We're family. I got you. I'll show you."

Still holding out my hand, Marlon accepted reluctantly. He gave me a slow handshake and it felt a bit untrusting. He walked me to the door. When I turned to walk out the door, I heard someone walking down the stairs. We both quickly turned around and watched her. She was so beautiful, but she wasn't my type. She seemed to be just like Suga, self-centered. But she was fuckable, just like Suga. Her round breasts bounced with each step and so did my dick.

"Dee, this is Santé, Suga's cousin," he said.

"Damn, you sure are fine," I said.

"Nice to see you again. We met at the party," she said.

She offered her hand for me to shake. Instead, I lifted her soft hand to my lips and kissed her hand. She gave me a slight smile and walked away. My eyes followed her every step of the way.

SNOOK

"What the fuck is she doing here?" I asked.

"She's visiting from New York. This is something her and Suga had already planned. That's the shit I'm talking about. Why would she tell Santé she could come here if she planned on leaving me? You know how jealous Suga is. She would never leave a woman in her house alone with me," he said.

I squeezed Marlon's shoulder on my way out. He loved her so much that he seemed lifeless without her. I once felt the same way about Kendra before she was taken away from me. I felt that same pain he was feeling watching my wife die in the hospital and leaving her body in a casket to be buried six feet under. I knew that pain all too well.

CHAPTER 7

Marlon

I tried to sort through the events of the day. The police showed up to our place of business accusing my wife of murdering her lesbian lover, my wife writes me a Dear John letter, and my best friend is acting suspiciously. I was starting not to trust Dee, especially since the stunt he pulled in the hospital when he made the sly comment about my son looking like him. It fucked with me so much that I needed a DNA test to confirm that Junior was really mine. I was in deep thought when Santé called out for me.

"Hey, is your friend gone?" she asked.

I joined her in the kitchen. She was searching the cabinets until she found a coffee mug.

"Want some?" she asked.

She waved the mug in my direction.

"Sure," I said.

She took two coffee mugs from the cabinet and turned on the coffee maker.

"I know that things are tough right now, but we have to put our heads together. I know my cousin and I don't think she would've left you or Junior," she said.

I didn't respond to her statements. I felt that she knew more than she led on. If Suga trusted anyone, it was Santé. I decided to stay quiet and let her talk. We sat quietly at the table until the coffee was ready.

She poured us both a cup of coffee and joined me at the table.

"I love my cousin and I will never betray her. But in this case, I have to tell you something. If Suga really left, it wasn't planned. She and I had some business together and I know she wouldn't have left without seeing me first," she said.

"What business did you two have?" I asked.

"That's between Suga and me."

"That business wouldn't involve the tubs she took from her father's house when Trey tried to kill her. I found them in my garage; one is full of cash. What the hell do you know about that?"

Santé's eyes widened. She tripped over her words.

"Cash? What cash? I don't know anything about a tub of cash?"

"What else was in the tubs?"

"I don't know what you're talking about? She didn't tell me nothing about money."

"Whatever secret alliance you had with her is dead now! Suga is gone!"

Santé began to cry.

"I don't know where she is. Maybe she needed a break or something. Somebody tried to kill her in front of her child. She may be having a mental breakdown. You know how fragile she can be. She's been through so much with her mother dying and her aunt," she said through tears.

"I don't want to sound insensitive, but I don't give a fuck about your tears. If you're going to be here, you have to help me find Suga. If you know something, tell me. I have to find my wife. She's wanted for murder."

"Murder? Who she supposed to have murdered?"

"The police came to the store earlier and told me that Suga murdered L.C. and her girlfriend. I know she didn't do it," I said.

"Damn right she didn't do it. She ain't no murderer! Where did they get that from?"

"It's a long story. After the visit from the police, I rushed here and found her letter."

"I know that Suga didn't hurt anybody. I don't know how they think she would do something like that. Poor Suga… Do you think that's why she could've ran?"

"It's a possibility, but I don't think that's it. Why would she leave all that money in the garage? Why did she wreck our bedroom? Shit just not adding up."

"But she did write the letter, right?"

"I'm almost positive of that. I know her handwriting. This shit is unreal!"

I slammed my fist down on the table.

Santé reached across the table and placed her soft hands over my fist. I looked at her.

"Everything is going to be all right. We're going to find her and when we do, we can both take turns kicking her ass for putting us through all of this," she said, half-jokingly. "If you don't mind, Ali will be down in a couple of days."

"It's fine. He's more than welcome here. I can't stand to be in this house alone. I know that you need his support as well."

"Thank you, Marlon."

I moved my hand away from hers. She looked surprised.

"Sorry," she said.

I gave a small laugh.

"I have to get this place cleaned up and figure out what my next move is going to be," I said.

"Don't worry about it. I can do it. You need to see your son and gather your thoughts. I can take care of the house," she said.

"Are you sure? Junior is going to stay with my mom until I get this figured out."

"Yeah, that's a good idea. But go to your son and find some peace. I will be here when you get back. If anything happens, I'll call you."

I took a few deep breaths.

"Okay. You have my number, right?" I asked.

"Of course," she said.

"Lock the doors behind me and set the alarm. I'll write the code down for you. Don't open the door for nobody, not even Dee if he comes back. I'll talk to him later," I said.

I handed her the paper with the security code to the alarm. She looked at me suspiciously, but complied with my request. I headed out to my mother's house to see my son. Just the thought of seeing his face and holding him close to my heart gave me some hope. Although my heart was aching for Suga, it was also yearning for my son.

As I drove to my parents' house, I was anxious to see my son. I fidgeted in my seat unable to settle in for the drive. I gripped the steering wheel hard, causing my hands to cramp. The last few months' events played in my mind. First the drama with Kendra; we'd slept together and she claimed that we'd conceived a child. She blackmailed me for money in the form of child support. I agreed to pay in order to keep her mouth closed. I did everything I could to keep that secret from Suga. If she was to find out that I had sex with her best friend and that her goddaughter was my child, I knew she would leave me. At the end, what's done in the dark always came to the light. Suga found out what happened and I found out that Kendra lied about me being her daughter's father.

The thing that haunted me the most is what I did to Suga in the hospital. It was my fault that she ran and was almost killed. If I hadn't treated her the way I did after having our son, Teesa would be alive and Suga wouldn't have almost lost her life. Worst of all, my son witnessed everything at only a few days old. As my thoughts raced in my mind, I had to clear my head. I was around the corner from my parent's house and I pulled over so that I could get myself together. I didn't want to alarm them. I surely didn't want to have negative energy around my son.

I visited with my son. I held Junior and kissed him. Looking into his eyes let me know that everything was going to be all right. I spent a few hours with him; changing his diapers, feeding him and holding him as he slept was comforting. My mother was very concerned. She knew that something was wrong. I was able to convince her that she needed to keep Junior for a couple of days. Saying bye to my son was hard. I didn't know what the next couple of days had in store for me. I was determined more than ever to bring Suga back home.

Suga

My head throbbed as I tried to adjust my eyes to the darkness in the room. It seemed as if hours had passed and I was waking up from a very long deep sleep. My head was swimming as I tried to grasp reality. In my mind, I was scared, panicking, and screaming for help but my body was calm. I felt high. I looked around, but couldn't make much of where I was. I tried to speak, but found that my mouth was gagged. I tried to push the gag out of my mouth, but it didn't bulge. My mouth was so dry that I felt the sides of my mouth split at my attempt. I tried to move, but found my hands bound behind my back. I wasn't sure where I was. I could see that it was night from a small window across the room.

I forced myself to focus because I knew I was in an unfamiliar place. I could see what looked like the side of a house; shrubbery obstructed my full view as well as my position. I tried to sit up, but a pain in my hip caused me to lay back down. I was stiff from laying in the same position for too long and that was bad for my hip injury. All of a sudden, my back began to spasm; another result of my injuries from Trey's attempt on my life. I knew I had to sit up in order to try to get to my feet. I took in a deep breath and fought through the pain. I slowly lifted my upper body to a sitting position. My head began to pound. I closed my eyes tightly. I waited a few moments for the pain to subside.

The dank mildew smell made me think that I was in a basement or an old building. I had to get out of here. I scooted back until I felt a cold wall. Lifting my legs to scoot was painful. Tears fell from my eyes. I didn't let the pain discourage me. Once my back was against the wall, I allowed myself a moment to compose myself. I knew my hardest task was in front me; standing to my feet. I would normally need my cane to stand and walk. I pulled my knees up and used the wall to support me. I managed to use the wall to support my weight. With all the strength I had in me, I pushed myself to my feet. All the while, my legs shook and my hip screamed out in pain. That one side was so weak and painful that it felt like all the strength came from the other side. I thought about my son and that was where the strength came from. My legs wobbled and I felt faint. I slid down the wall, back onto the floor and into the darkness.

My head pounded, forcing me to squeeze my eyes shut. I was groggy and didn't know where I was or how I'd gotten there. I could hear water dripping slowly at three-second intervals. I remember a bumpy ride as I floated in and out of consciousness. I tried to fight through a headache to recall what led to me being in an unfamiliar place, and then I remembered what happened.

After dropping off Marlon Jr. at my mother in law's house, I returned home to plan a nice quiet evening for me and Marlon. I made reservations for dinner and I purchased new lingerie for later. We needed some alone time. Although we enjoyed our beautiful bundle of joy, a new baby at home was a lot for the both of us to get used to.

When I returned home and pulled into the driveway there was a dark vehicle with tinted windows sitting on the street. I proceeded to pull into the driveway, watching the rearview as I paid attention to the vehicle driving by. Shutting off my car and gathering my bags from the front seat, I heard a car pull in behind me and beep the horn. I assumed it was Marlon. I smiled, gathered my things, and leaped out of the car.

"Hey, babe…" I began to say.

The smile on my face fell into a frown when I saw Dee standing before me with a wild look in his eyes.

"Hey, baby," he said. "Stay calm and go in the house."

"What do you think you're doing? Marlon will be here in a minute. So whatever you think you're going to accomplish isn't going to happen."

He stepped closer to me, invading my personal space and said, "Get your ass in the house, now! Or I can do you right here. It doesn't matter to me."

He lifted his shirt to show me that he was armed. I dropped my bags and tried to run, but he grabbed me.

"Get your hands off of me! Let me go!" I shouted.

He dug his nails into my arms.

"Shut the fuck up! I don't have time for this. Let's go," he said.

He picked up the bags that I dropped without letting go of my arm and walked me to the house. I knew that Marlon wasn't expected to be home for a couple of hours and I needed to make him think that he would be home at any minute.

"If Marlon catch you here, what do you think he's going to do?" I asked.

"You don't get it, do you? I don't give a fuck about Marlon or you! Now open the damn door!"

I struggled to find the house key, but I managed to find it. I fumbled with the lock, dropping the keys. My hands were shaking uncontrollably. I didn't know what he wanted or what he would do once we were inside. He pushed me down to pick up the keys and then yanked them out of my hand. He opened the door and shoved me inside.

"Ouch!" I screamed, falling to the floor. My handbag and shopping bags flew across the floor.

Dee slammed the door behind us. He quickly assessed the house because he scanned the nearby rooms. I pulled myself off the floor.

"You're coming with me," Dee said.

"What? I'm not going anywhere with you. Are you crazy?"

"Hell yeah, I'm crazy! I'm crazy about you," Dee said sarcastically.

"Oh my God! You're crazy. I will never be with you. You will never be the man that Marlon is."

"Don't flatter yourself bitch, this ain't want you think it is. Do what the fuck I tell you to do or I'm going to save myself the trouble and do you right now," he said.

I quickly came up with a plan to grab the first weapon I could find to fight for my life. I decided to do what he wanted.

"Come on," he said as he shoved me towards the stairs.

I slowly walked towards the stairs with Dee right behind me.

When we reached the top of the stairs he said, "Go to your room and pack some clothes. Hurry up!"

I went to my room and quickly grabbed a suitcase and began throwing anything I could get my hands on, yanking and pulling clothes off of the hangers. Some fell to the floor and some made it into the suitcase.

While I was in the closet, I could hear Dee rummaging through things. After the suitcase was filled, I dragged it out of the closet. I saw my makeup bag on the dresser. Dee sat on my bed with the gun pointed at me. I moved over to my dresser. I eyed a tube of lipstick and thought about writing a message to Marlon if I could get to it.

"Stand right there and don't move. I'm telling you Suga, don't fuck with me."

He jumped off the bed, walked into my closet, and began yanking things off the hangers. Then he walked over to my dresser and knocked everything on the floor.

We walked back downstairs to the kitchen. I watched Dee rummage through the kitchen drawers looking for something. He finally pulled out a small notebook and ink pen. He placed the paper and pen on the counter. He turned towards me with the gun, waving it at me.

"Come over here. Write Marlon a convincing letter telling him you're leaving him," he said.

"But I'm not leaving him. You're taking me away from

him, you sick son of a bitch!" I screamed.

I launched at him with my hands flying wildly. He backhanded me, sending me flying into the counter. I scrambled for the nearest thing I could reach, the coffee pot. I grabbed the coffee pot and went to fling it towards Dee. He grabbed my hand, took the coffee pot out of my hand, and placed it back on the counter and he put the gun against my forehead.

"Try something like that again and I'll make sure you bury your son," he said.

I let out a cry for my child. I had to do what he wanted for the sake of my child.

"Tell him you're leaving and make it believable!" he shouted.

I wrote my last words to my husband. I was hoping that he wouldn't believe any of it. I needed him to see past the words and into my heart. I wanted him to believe that I would never leave him or our son. As I was writing the letter, I had an idea. I needed to secretly pen a message to Marlon without Dee knowing.

After I finished the letter, I pretended to look over it. I lifted the paper and placed my pen underneath it on the next sheet of paper.

"Read it," he said.

I read him the letter slowly. As I read the letter, I moved the pen under the paper, writing the words, *Help Dee.* That was all I could write before he shoved me. He picked up the notebook and read it for himself. He ripped the letter from the notebook. I prayed that he wouldn't see my message. He didn't and I breathed a sigh of relief. He placed the letter on the refrigerator held by a magnet. The last thing I remember was Dee forcing me to drink from a water bottle.

Just when I thought I was getting my life together and moving forward in my marriage with Marlon, I was taken from my home at gunpoint. I was forced to write a letter to Marlon making him think that I had left him for good.

I must be in the lower level of a building or house because I could hear footsteps above me. I had no way to tell what time it was. I knew that I did some fucked up shit in the past, but I was truly committed to him and our family. Nothing or nobody was ever going to change that. The thought of my son sent tears running down my face gathering in my ears. I didn't know what was happening or why it was happening. First, I was pistol-whipped, went into a coma, and now I was abducted.

I heard footsteps above me. The floor above creaked under the weight of someone. I began to shake and hyperventilate. Up until now, he didn't hurt me. I assumed that he was waiting for something or somebody.

Why wouldn't he just kill me? What was he waiting for?

Trying to push the gag out of my mouth, I rubbed my head back and forth, forcing what was tied around my mouth to slide down enough so that I could maneuver and spit out the gag. I fought to catch my breath. My first thought was to scream. I didn't know what was going to happen next. Either way, I was going to make some noise. If it was my time to die, I wasn't going to lay on my back and wait.

"Help! Help! Help me! Please! Help me!" I shouted.

I waited to see if I heard anything. I didn't hear anything.

"Help me! Somebody please!" I called out.

SNOOK

Tears ran down my face as I begged, screamed, and squirmed. All I knew was that I had to get away. If this was my chance, I wasn't going to let my opportunity slip away. If someone was up there with him, they were going to know that I was down here. I stopped screaming to listen. I didn't hear anything. No footsteps, no voices.

Towards the left of me, a loud rumbling noise echoed. I turned my head toward the noise and saw a furnace and hot water heater. The fire underneath the heater showed blue and lit the small corner with light. Besides the light through the small window, the room was dark; it was getting late. Marlon was going to be home soon. I knew he would come looking for me; help had to be on the way soon.

I didn't know what was going on in Dee's mind. I made it clear to him that Marlon was the love of my life and I chose my family. The affair we had was out of hurt and anger and nothing more. Somehow, he didn't understand. Even after he forced himself on me at my party, I never thought that he would do something like this.

Heavy footsteps clobbered over me. I heard the volume of a television go up to a level loud enough to drown out my screams. I listened to the footsteps as they crossed from near the window across the room, then the footsteps stopped. The hair on the back of my neck stood up. Just as I was about to let out another scream, I heard a door open. A grinding metal echoed through the silence. The scream caught in my throat as fear forced a hard cough. My heart sped up and I shook uncontrollably. The door creaked open. I turned to look towards the stairs.

"God, please let that be someone here to help me. I don't want to die like this," I said through my tears.

The door swung open and hit the wall. I heard him before I saw him. He rushed down the stairs and suddenly stopped.

"You bitch!" Dee said.

He didn't look like the Dee I knew. He was out of his mind. He looked at me in disgust as I cried out.

"Why are you doing this to me?" I yelled.

"Why are you making all this noise? All that screaming and shit. Nobody is going to hear you down here. Nobody is coming for you. You're just irritating the hell out of me!" Dee spat.

He was still standing four feet away from me.

"What do you want from me? Is it money you want? I can get you money," I said.

He walked slowly towards me. The closer he came towards me the heavier fear sat on my chest. He stopped in front of me.

"I want you to shut the fuck up. Nobody is going to hear you down here!" he yelled.

His eyes were so cold. His tone so vacant. I had no doubt that he would hurt me. I tried to calm myself. He reached over me and I flinched. He laughed at me. He loosened the ties that bound my hands and they fell to the floor. I quickly pulled my arms towards the front of my body. He examined my wrists that were rubbed raw. I held my bleeding wrists against my shirt. I kept an eye on Dee as he walked over to the opposite side of the room.

"Do you have to go to the bathroom?" he asked, holding open the door.

I hadn't thought about food or relieving myself until then. I stood up slowly, legs weak. It took me a minute to get to my feet on my own. As soon as I stood, I felt how full my bladder was. I made my way in the dark towards the bathroom. I walked inside and turned towards him, waiting for him to close the door.

"Can I have some privacy, please?" I asked calmly.

"You don't have nothing I haven't fucked before. Use it or forget it," he said.

I looked at him with disgust.

He held the door as I used the bathroom. He watched my every move, making me uncomfortable. When I was done he led me back. He tied my arms behind my back and sat me up against the wall.

"I'll be back," he said.

He slowly backed away from me and then turned around and jogged back up the stairs. He slammed the door and locked it. I didn't know what horror he had planned for me. I prayed that Marlon would figure it all out. If only he saw my message, he would see that things weren't as they seemed.

CHAPTER 9

Linwood

The noisy recreation room began to drown out my thoughts of self-pity. I was sitting with four other inmates at a table. Ben, who was a talented artist, was drawing my self-portrait. He could draw and paint with the best of them. He was on that Picasso shit. He once drew a picture depicting the black family. It showed how the absence of the father impacted the family and I swear it brought tears to my eyes.

I was leaving soon and he wanted to give me a parting gift. I sat stone-faced as usual, never leading anyone to what I was thinking or how I felt. I found myself drifting off. I sat back in my chair. I thought about the dream I'd had the night before.

I awoke in a cold sweat. Sweat clung to my neck and chest and dripped down my face. My heart pounded in my chest. I sat up and tried to shake off the nightmare that I had. I wasn't a person to experience many dreams, but when I did it had to mean something. The other dreams were ones that I couldn't recall once I'd awaken. This dream was still clear in my mind.

In this dream, I was fighting two lions; one had the face of Teesa and the other Trey. They both attacked me at the same time. Teesa was on my back tearing at my skin screaming, "Why did you do this to me?" Trey was attacking me from the front, slashing at me. I grabbed Trey and slung him to the ground, breaking his back; he didn't move. From the corner of my eye, I saw another lion approaching me. This one had the face of Sable, Teesa's twin sister. She walked towards us slowly as Teesa slowly crawled off my back. Sable was the seductive one. The mole on her face was a dead giveaway. Teesa was no longer aggressive and she was also seducing me alongside her sister. I backed away from them. Both of their eyes turned crimson red and dripped bloody tears. They both pounced on me, knocking me to the ground. I held each one off with a hand around their necks. Their large sharp teeth came down towards me as they thundered the most ear piercing roar I'd ever heard. Then I woke up.

I knew what the dream meant because I had very similar ones involving both Teesa and Sable but never had I dreamed about Trey along with the two of them. Teesa and Sable were my karma. I'd betrayed Teesa and slept with her identical twin sister, Sable. That ripped the life from Teesa. The same night she found out about Sable was the night she found out I had a wife. My karma was in full effect from there.

When Redd came for a visit unexpectedly, I knew

something was wrong. He told me that the woman I grieved for, wasn't Teesa, it was Sable. Teesa killed Sable, stole her identity, and abandoned our daughter. He told me that Trey killed Teesa and almost killed Suga because of me. He wanted my money. Needless to say that the visit was cut short after I blacked out and cleared the visiting room.

I knew I was wrong for not telling Teesa that I had a wife. But I knew she wasn't the type of woman to share her man with another woman so I hid the truth from her. When I started making a lot of money, I began to make fucked up decisions. I had women throwing themselves at me all the time, especially at my place of business. I knew I was going to have to pay for my sins eventually. When the government came for me, I knew I was going to burn.

I was adding up the numbers in my mind. I needed to know what to expect when I got home. There was the money in my safe deposit box that only I had access to and in the event of my death, Suga would inherit everything. Then there was the cash and merchandise in the attic of my home. That was the money that cost Teesa her life and almost the life of my daughter.

"Seems like you have something heavy on your head. You good, Wood?" Ben asked.

"I'm good," I said.

"You're going home soon, you should be wearing a smile in this pic. A lot of us wish that we were going home to our families. Some of us will never see them streets again," Ben said. He stopped drawing and looked behind me.

"Wood, I need to talk to you," Lamar said.

"What's up?" I asked

"Kyle."

I followed Lamar to our cell. Lamar stood guard as I retrieved the cell from its hiding place. I looked over my shoulder to be sure that it was safe to talk.

"What's up?" I said.

"How are you doing, man?" Kyle asked.

"I'll be better if you had good news for me."

"I have some good news for you. I was able to get the judge to sign off on your release."

"Good! How soon are we talking?"

"You should be released no later than tomorrow. The paperwork has to go through the proper channels. That, I have no control over. We've jumped through the biggest hurdle and that was the release papers."

"Thanks for getting that done."

"No problem. Now you know that you still have some outstanding fees with me…"

"I'll pay you, don't worry about that."

"I know you will."

"You just do what I pay you for and we won't have no problems."

Kyle cleared his throat and paused.

"I'll see you when you come home. Do you need a ride home?"

"No, I have a friend that's coming to pick me up."

"A friend… Is it the friend that you told me about? The one that you were pen pals with."

"Yeah, her name is Mona. She'll be here to pick me up."

"Make sure you let me know when you touch down. Talk to you soon."

I didn't say anything to that. I just hung up the phone. I was going to see him when I got home, no doubt about that. I was going to make him pay for every day that I spent behind bars and for every dollar he stole from me. He was going to pay for the time I didn't have with Suga and Teesa. Kyle and that dirty judge screwed me out of my deal.

CHAPTER 10

Santé

I rolled over in the bed almost forgetting where I was. It was the best sleep that I had in a very long time. I was sure that Suga spared no expense on the memory foam pillows and goose down comforter. The mattress had to have been one of those expensive ones because it felt like I was sleeping on clouds. The bed felt so good that I didn't want to get out.

Reality quickly set in as the emptiness of the house was not to be denied. I began to feel out of place. I sat up in the bed when I heard the sound of the doorbell. I wasn't sure if or when Marlon came home.

I quickly jumped out of bed and ran out of the bedroom. I quickly glanced into Suga and Marlon's bedroom. It didn't appear that the bed had been slept in. I ran down the stairs wondering where Marlon was. Marlon met me at the bottom of the stairs. He was in the same clothes he had on yesterday.

I looked in the living room and saw a blanket thrown across the arm of the sofa.

"Good morning," he said.

I intentionally looked him in the eyes to see if he would look away. He made eye contact. All I saw in his eyes was pain. I was beginning to feel that maybe he didn't have anything to do with Suga's disappearance.

"Good morning. Are you expecting anyone?" I asked.

"No," he said.

The doorbell rung again. I followed Marlon to the front door. He swung the door open wide.

"Oh my, God!" I screamed.

"Hey, baby!" Ali said.

I ran and jumped into his arms almost knocking him down. I wrapped my legs and arms around him. Ali held me with his muscular arms and kissed me deeply. When he put me down, I noticed that he wasn't alone. Standing outside of the car was Queenie, Raheem, and Dirt.

"I wasn't expecting you. You said you were sending Queenie." I playfully tapped him on his shoulder.

"She's here," Ali said.

"Come on in," Marlon said. He followed me in the house.

Since the two of them never met, Marlon was watching us. Although they were meeting under unusual circumstances for the first time, I introduced them.

"Ali, this is Marlon," I said.

"What's up?" Ali asked.

"We finally get to meet. How are you?" Marlon asked.

The two of them shook hands.

"Where is your cousin? Do I get to finally meet her?" Ali asked.

He knew Suga was gone. I looked at him as if he'd lost his mind. He looked at me as if he really expected an answer.

"She isn't here," I said.

"My wife is missing. I'm not sure where she is," Marlon said.

I turned towards Marlon, who was looking as if he was ready to cry.

"Yeah, she's missing. We're here trying to figure things out," I said.

"Sorry to hear that. Did you call the police?" Ali asked.

His eyes were glued on Marlon.

"If I don't hear anything today, I'm going to call them," Marlon said.

"Marlon, you can talk to Ali. He can help us, trust me," I told him.

The house phone rang and time seemed to stand still. I didn't breathe for a brief moment. Marlon dashed for the phone with both me and Ali on his heels. He yanked the phone off the base.

"Hello?" he answered. He sounded loud and winded.

I watched in anticipation, praying that it was Suga. Marlon's facial expression went from one of pain to disappointment.

"She's not here," he said.

I breathed out my disappointment.

"Santé is here. Would you like to speak to her?" he asked.

Marlon handed me the phone.

"Who is it?" I whispered.

I took the phone from him. He twisted his mouth but didn't answer.

"Hello?"

"Hey, Santé! How's my favorite niece?" Uncle Linwood asked.

"Hey, Unc! I'm fine. I'm glad you called."

I covered the phone and told Ali and Marlon that I was taking the phone call upstairs. Marlon's eyes pleaded with me not to disclose the current situation but I ignored him. I kissed Ali on the cheek and took the call to the guest room.

"Listen, Suga is missing. We don't know where she is. It looks like somebody took her," I said.

"Fuck! Somebody took my daughter? Bitches keep coming for my family!" he said.

I could hear his voice fade off in the distance.

"Unc, please don't get this call ended. I really need to talk to you."

"What the fuck Marlon into? He had to have fucked somebody over for them to take her. They want something. Did he get a ransom call?"

"Not yet. Don't worry. My boyfriend, Ali, is here. He's going to make sure that Marlon is on the up and up about what's going on. If there is anything he can do to get Suga back home I know he's going to do it. I got my eye on Marlon for now. I'm not sure what or how much he has to do with this. I know that Suga didn't leave on her own because she knew I was coming to town. I have something that she needs. I know she wouldn't have left without it," I said.

"Oh, okay. I see what you're saying. Yeah, something ain't right," he said.

"If you can call back as often as you can, I'll keep you updated."

"I may not need to call because I'm coming home today. I'm just waiting for them to come get me."

"Really? How?"

"Don't worry about that. Just know I'll be home. I gotta get home to Suga. My baby has been through too much for things to turn out like this."

"Don't worry, I'll do everything I can to get her back."

"I have to go. I was calling to see if Suga could pick me up because my girlfriend can't get off in time. I need you to pick me up. Can you do that?"

"Of course. What time?"

"Be here by ten o'clock."

"Okay. I love you. See you soon."

"I love you, too."

I was happy to hear that my uncle was coming home early. That news was right on time. With Ali and Linwood, there was no way we could fail at getting Suga back. I had to know one thing; if I could trust Marlon.

CHAPTER 11

Marlon

After Santé ran off with the phone, I was left with Ali. This was my first time meeting him, but I'd heard about him. He had respect in the streets. Although he was from New York, he was well known in Virginia. His associates were also well known and feared. Being that I didn't have anyone other than Dee to lean on in this situation, I knew I needed all the help I could get. Right now, I had to give him a chance. I hoped that with Santé's love for Suga, he would do right by us.

"Do you want something to drink? I have a few cold beers," I said.

With all the excitement, I could use a drink.

"I'll take one if you're having one," Ali said.

I retrieved the beers and we went into the living room to talk. At first, it was awkward. I opened my beer and begin to sip it. Ali sat his beer down without opening it.

"Tell me what you know so far about this. I might be able to give you some insight," Ali said.

"Suga and I had some issues lately. We were working things out and things seemed to be getting better. You know she had the incident and her mother died. Yesterday, detectives showed up at the store, talking about Suga set me up for the murder of her friend. I didn't believe them. I tried to call her after that and couldn't reach her by phone. So I came home and she wasn't here. I found a letter talking about she was leaving. After checking the house, it was clear that she was taken."

"Shit," Ali said.

"I couldn't make this shit up. That's the story in a nutshell."

"If she was taken, who do you think would've wanted to take her? What do you think they want?"

"I'm not sure if this has anything to do with Linwood or not. Trey came for him, but I don't think so. This is something else."

"What about competition? Any issues with business partners? Anyone you may have crossed?"

"No, that's why it doesn't make sense."

Out of nowhere Ali said, "I believe you."

"What the fuck are you talking about?"

Ali sat back deeper into the sofa and said, "I said I believe you. I don't think you know where Suga is. See, I have a gift. I can see through the bullshit. I've been watching you since I got here. I've been watching your eyes and your body language. I know a liar when I see one. Most of all, I know when to trust someone. I trust you."

I let out a small chuckle. I sat my beer down and leaned forward placing my elbows on my knees.

"What the fuck you mean you believe me! I don't care what you've been watching. I don't give a fuck if you believed me or not," I said.

I stood to my feet. His arrogant ass didn't flinch. He picked up his beer and opened it.

"Who the fuck do you think you are coming in here…" I started to say before being rudely cut off by Ali.

Ali stood to his feet and said, "I don't give a fuck about you. I love what Santé loves, and she loves your wife. I'm making it my business to make sure that I do what I can to make sure that she is found."

"I don't give a fuck about you either. You can get the fuck out my house! I didn't ask you for your help. I can find my wife on my own."

"I don't see anyone else here with you. I don't see your boys here with you trying to figure this shit out. I'm not here to fight with you. I'm here to help. I have my family here with me, we can help you. Fuck it. We can work together or we can work against each other. It's up to you."

I was ready to throw Ali out on his ass. He was right, I didn't have many people to turn to for help in this situation. I knew a lot of people in the streets and in business, but I didn't know who I could trust. Someone could've been trying to make some quick money or I had an enemy out there.

Ali held out his hand and said, "We all want the same thing, we want Suga to return home safely. Right?"

I debated on bashing Ali in the head with my beer bottle

or accepting his help. Help was what I needed. I had to find her and bring her back home to our son.

"All right, man," I said.

I reluctantly accepted his hand and we shook on it.

"I got you. We're going to find her," he said.

"I have to find my baby. This shit is crazy!"

"Sorry, but I had to be sure that you weren't trying to run game on me. The first suspect was you. A smart man like you already knew that."

Santé entered the room and stood between us and held my arm. "Marlon, it's okay... We had to be sure that you didn't have anything to do with this," she said.

At first, Ali came off arrogant and cocky. When I shook his hand and looked into eyes I saw the sincerity in his eyes. I knew then he was testing me to see if he could trust me. With everything that was happening in my life, it seemed as though I couldn't get off of the roller coaster. Everything I did from here on out was about my family and I was determined to do whatever it took to get my family back. What I wouldn't give to hold Suga again and look into her beautiful face.

"Hey, man. Do you mind if my team come in and put our heads together on this?" Ali asked.

I didn't answer immediately. I sat deeper in my chair. I knew that I needed more help than I had at my disposal. Dee was my ear to the streets. My cousins would be the last people I call when it's time for gunplay.

"Don't feel like you're in this alone. You're family now. Trust me, if it's something we can do to help bring her home, we're going to do it. Anything," Ali said.

I looked at Ali and nodded my approval.

Ali placed a call on his cell phone. In a matter of seconds, the doorbell rang.

Santé opened the door.

In walked the most unusual trio I'd ever seen. I stood to greet the team.

Ali walked over to where they stood.

"This is Queenie, Raheem, and Dirt. This is my team, but we are more like a family," Ali said.

"Hello. Thanks for coming down in a time like this," I said.

I shook each person's hand as we greeted each other.

Queenie was cute but in a tomboyish way. She was brown-skinned, petite and had a mouth full of gold teeth. Her small stature made her appear non-threatening, but in her eyes, I saw a monster. Her hair was in small dreads dyed blonde at the ends

Raheem was tall, dark, muscular and clean-cut. I expected him to have a very deep voice for a man of his stature, but it wasn't. His hands were huge. His grip was strong enough to break every bone in my hand if he tried.

Dirt was young. He had a baby face, but there was an edge about him. He had a hunger in his eyes that reminded me of the hunger I used to see in Dee. He wore his hair in an afro and baggy clothes.

It was an odd crew, but I was sure that each wheel moved the vehicle. I offered them a seat as I sat back down. I noticed that Queenie and Dirt sat very close to each other. Raheem stood beside Ali. All eyes were on me.

"As you already know my wife is missing. The short version is that she was taken. She was forced to write me a letter saying that she was leaving me. After checking the house, I realized that she couldn't have left on her own free will. Right now, I got my boy, Dee, out there trying to find out what the streets know. I have Gooch and my cousins for when things get heated. I don't want to call them in just yet," I said.

"Is there anyone that wants to hurt you or your family? Who are your enemies?" Raheem asked.

"I've had a few problems in the past; none of them would've come at me like this. There could be a jealous competitor out there. I have a few successful jewelry stores and some folks aren't happy about that," I said.

"You don't always know your enemies. They could be your friends or your family. Never count anyone out. Coming for your heart is personal," Raheem said.

"We have to look at those closest to you and Suga," Ali said.

I didn't respond because they were right. Dee was weighing heavy on my mind. I knew that what they were saying was true. It's more than likely the one that's closest to you that sticks the knife in your back. If I had to choose the one person that would turn on me, Dee would be that person.

"Fuck friends right now. You need to look at everybody in your circle and eliminate them one by one," Dirt said.

"Who do you trust? Let's start there. I've seen this happen so many times," Queenie added.

I didn't know what to say. I didn't want to look like a fool and throw Dee's name out there after I'd just said that he was out there looking for Suga. My stomach flipped at the thought of Dee having something to do with Suga's disappearance. I shook off the thought.

"I have a few people that I trust. I don't see too many of them coming at me like this," I said.

"Marlon, I don't mean no disrespect. What's up with Dee? I know he's your boy and all, but I never trusted him. When he came over, I felt that something wasn't right with him. He looks very sneaky and conniving. Do you think he could have something to do with all of this?" Santé asked.

Everyone in the room seemed to agree with Santé by the sound of grunts and sighs.

"That's my boy. We came up together. He recently lost his wife, Kendra. She and Suga were best friends," I said.

"How did she die?" Queenie asked.

"She was killed. Somebody kicked in and shot them both. He was the only one to survive. We still don't know who did it," I said.

"Is he in the drug game?" Ali asked.

"He do his thing," I said.

"So, Dee is looking like our man. We need to see him," Ali said.

I shook my hand in disagreement, as I tried to accept the fact that there was a possibility that Dee could be behind this. I had to share my thoughts on the situation.

"To be honest, I don't think he had anything to do with this. He's like a brother to me," I said.

"Have you and Dee had any problems in the past? Is there anything you can think of?" Ali asked.

"We've had our problems in the past. He's been through

some things and at one time…" I paused as anger filled my body. I hated the words that were about to escape my lips, but it had to be said. "One time, I thought that he and Suga were having an affair," I said.

"What? Suga wouldn't let him touch her with a ten-foot pole!" Santé said.

"Look, I had my suspicions. He implied that my son was his. He did that right in my face at the hospital. He tried to make it look like a joke, but I didn't find shit funny. That was why I had a paternity test on my son as soon as that happened. Suga was acting all funny and shit when he came around. They were acting too weird around each other," I said.

The room went silent. It was so much heavy information dropped, that I was sure they were trying to keep up. I looked at Santé, who I was sure knew just as much as I was telling them. My cell phone rang, getting all of our attention.

"It's a private number," I said. I looked at my phone strangely. I knew that it was someone blocking their number. The hair on the back of my neck stood up and my stomach sunk.

"Here we go. That's the call right there. I put money on it," Raheem said.

CHAPTER 12

Dee

Smoke filled my bedroom as I laid between the legs of Lex as she smoked a blunt. As badly as I wanted to send her outside to smoke, I didn't want her to leave me alone. We laid in the bed that I shared with Kendra. She rubbed my back and gave me a sense of comfort that I hadn't felt in a very long time. I'd met Lex at a grief counseling session at my sister's church. Chrissy convinced me to attend the meetings. I can't say that the few meetings I did attend didn't help, but I wasn't as receptive to it as I should've been. One good thing that came out of the class was meeting Lex. She'd lost her husband to cancer. We both met in our sorrow and used sex to deal with our pain.

"What's wrong, baby? Is something on your mind tonight?" Lex asked.

"It is. I have something I need to do later," I said.

"Well let's not let that get in the way of what we have to do now."

She passed me the blunt. I sat up and moved beside her. Lex separated a few lines of cocaine. She leaned over the nightstand and inhaled a couple lines. I watched her as I puffed on the blunt. I'd already had my fix and was flying high.

Lex spread her thick, shapely thighs. She rubbed her hands over her smooth brown skin. She rubbed herself, dipping her fingers in and out of herself. She moaned with pleasure, making my dick hard. I stroked my dick as I watched. She removed a finger and sucked it. She placed a wet finger in the cocaine. She slowly lowered her cocaine covered finger down to her sweet spot and inserted her finger, her finger went in and out. She grinded her hips against her hand and used her other hand to squeeze her nipples. My eyebrows raised in curiosity. I'd never seen anyone do something like that.

She motioned with a wet dripping finger for me to come to her. No words were needed to be spoken, I knew what she wanted, and I gave it to her. After we fucked, Lex passed out. That gave me time to handle some business that I'd been putting off.

I slid out of bed, careful not to wake up Lex. I grabbed a small bag from under the bed and took it to the bathroom with me. Inside was a burner phone and a voice recorder. I'd been thinking all day about what my message should be. I didn't want a long dragged out message, but I needed the message to be taken seriously. I quietly rehearsed the message over and over until I felt it was good enough. When I was finally satisfied, I became nervous again. I knew once I did this, there was no turning back. It was game time. I was already at the point of no return, but this would set the wheels in motion to getting what I wanted. I pressed the record button and spoke in a very deep voice in an attempt to disguise my voice as much as possible.

"I have your wife. If you want her back, I want half a million in cash on Thursday. I'll call you with the time and the place. Call the police and your bitch is dead."

I ended the recording and listened to it. I was satisfied with it and confident that I didn't sound like myself. I waited for him to answer. The phone rang a few times. Right when I was ready to hang up, I heard Marlon's voice. I quickly pressed the play button and placed the recorder to the phone. I noticed my shaking hand and realized how nervous I was.

When the recording was over I placed the phone back to my ear. I heard Marlon say, "You bitches better not hurt her! You'll get your money."

I ended the call. A knock on the bathroom door startled me.

"What?" I yelled.

"What are you doing in there? I've been waiting for you to come out. I have to use the bathroom," Lex said.

"I'm coming."

I wondered how long she'd been outside my door. I hope she didn't hear anything that could potentially put her life in danger. My plan was mine alone and I didn't need any loose strings. I opened the door and she wasn't there. I found her back in the bed still lying in her nakedness. Her beautiful smile assured me that nothing had changed between us.

SNOOK

I had Suga and the message was delivered. My original plan to make her suffer and leave her floating in the James River, changed when I thought about how much money Marlon would pay for her. I had her write the letter to crush him and then her body was supposed to turn up. Instead, I decided to get paid and still leave her floating in the James. I could kill two birds with one stone. After Marlon had suffered to my satisfaction, I would finally put a bullet in his head. I've been itching to kill him since the day I caught him fucking Kendra. I was going to get my revenge once and for all on both Suga and Marlon.

CHAPTER 13

Suga

I blinked a few times trying to open my eyes. My head was swimming and I felt very heavy. I wanted badly to wake up from this nightmare. When I finally was able to keep my eyes open, my lids felt so heavy. I was laying on my back, looking up at a ceiling. I was no longer in the unfinished basement. I rolled over on my right side and felt the cold tiled floor on my arm. The cold tile shocked my system and awakened my senses. I heard metal scraping the floor. When I looked down, I saw a thick chain and lock wrapped around my ankle.

I realized that I was in the bathroom. I sat up slowly fighting back an agonizing headache and a dry mouth. I used the toilet as leverage to stand to my feet. That was when I noticed extreme stiffness in my hip. My range of motion had become limited. I had to adjust and push through the pain to stand to my feet. Once to my feet, I paused for a second to see how my hip would tolerate my weight. It stood painfully firm. The chain was short. It didn't allow me to go outside of the small bathroom.

The chain was tied to the metal plumbing under the sink. I yanked at the chain. It didn't budge. I tried to use my hands to undo the pipes. I didn't have the strength or tools to make them budge. I tried to slip out of the chain around my ankle. It was wrapped so tightly that I could barely squeeze a finger in between the chain and my skin.

I turned on the cold water. I cupped my hands under the water to collect enough to drink. I repeated this several times until I had my fill. I hadn't had anything to eat or drink and I feared dehydration. I splashed my face with water. I needed to wake up and come up with a plan to escape. I splashed my face with cold water until I felt I was completely awake. I wasn't sure what he was giving me to keep me sleep, but it had me extremely groggy. I couldn't sort through my thoughts in that state.

I had avoided looking in the mirror because I didn't want to face myself. I knew that I'd brought part of this on myself. Sleeping with Dee's crazy ass was the worst mistake I could've ever made. Now he turned on me and my family. It was all my fault. I didn't want my son to grow up without a mother like I did.

I slowly lifted my head and faced myself. I was trying to change for the better. I was no longer thinking about myself, I had my son. I wanted to trust Marlon. There were still some things that he didn't know about, but he didn't have to know everything. I was trying to start over; only if he was willing to be honest. Just when I decided to play fair, I found myself in another life or death situation.

As I stared in the mirror and thought about all the bad things that I'd done, I thought about my new family. I hadn't been able to enjoy my son and Marlon. It hadn't sunk in that my family was finally complete. Although God had blessed me with a child, I didn't appreciate his blessing. I was too selfish. When little Marlon's handsome face entered my mind, it lit a fire in me. I was determined to do something to escape.

I ran a finger over the scar on my head from my last brush with death. I survived one monster, I knew I could do it again. This time, I would not be at his mercy begging for my life. I was going to fight.

I removed a sock, placed it over my hand, and punched the mirror. Instantly, the glass shattered, cutting my hand through the sock. My hand bled, but I didn't feel any pain. My adrenaline was racing. I picked up the largest piece of glass with a sharp end. I removed my other sock and wrapped it around the glass to be sure that I didn't cut my hand any worse. I was sure to remove as much of the glass from the sink and floor. After I flushed the rest of the broken glass down the toilet, I was ready.

Once I secured the glass in my hand, I began to scream to the top of my lungs.

"Help! Please, somebody, help me!" I screamed.

I threw my body against the wall, rattled my chains and continued screaming. I wasn't sure if he was home or if he'd left. I continued to scream and throw my body against the wall causing as much noise as I could. On cue, I heard someone come down the stairs outside of the bathroom. I continued to scream. I placed the hand with glass behind my back. Dee appeared in the doorway.

"Shut the fuck up!" Dee said.

He stood in front me in his underwear and shirt. I figured he was up there sleep.

"Let me go you crazy bastard! What the fuck do you want from me?" I screamed.

"I want you to shut the fuck up before I shut you up," he said.

"Let me go!"

"Not until Marlon pays up. If he don't, then I would have no use for your loud mouth ass."

"Fuck you! Marlon is going to kill your ass when he finds out what you did to me."

The dead stare he gave me sent chills down my spine. I didn't back down.

"You know what, you're going to die. I'm going to watch you die. I had to watch Kendra die, not you. You couldn't even come to the hospital to see her. She suffered and you of all people should've been there by her side. You never know what your presence could've done for her. She loved you! You being there could've brought her out that coma. I was there combing her hair and talking to her. Where were you? You let her die!" he said. Spit flew from the corners of his mouth.

I realized that Dee wasn't just angry with Marlon. He blamed me for Kendra's death. When I did go see her, it was too late. I did feel guilty about waiting so long to see her. I promised myself that if I made it out alive, I was going to go to her grave and apologize.

"I didn't let her die," I said.

"I'm tired of your ass," he said.

Dee stepped into the bathroom. I prayed he wouldn't notice the broken mirror. He knelt down to unlock the padlock on the chain with a small key. I watched the chain fall off. For a brief moment, I didn't feel confident that I would be able to run upstairs. I quickly shook the doubt out of mind and continued to ride on the adrenaline. Right before Dee went to stand back up, I stabbed him in his back with the glass. The glass broke and he fell to the floor screaming in pain.

I leaped over his body, praying that he didn't catch me by the leg like in the movies. I ran out the bathroom. I made it to the stairs and didn't break my stride because I knew if I did, I wouldn't make it. At the top of the stairs, I tried to open the door. It didn't budge. I twisted the knob and pressed my body against it and it finally opened. I knew that the front door was dead bolted so I didn't want to waste time running towards the front door. I turned towards the kitchen and headed for the back patio door. It felt as if I was being chased by pit bulls chomping at my ankles, although there was no one or nothing running behind me. Fear danced around me. I knew that I had to get out now. I knew that was my last chance to get free. If I didn't get out, I was not going to have another opportunity.

Entering the space that Kendra once inhabited hit me hard. I haven't been inside their home in a long time. To be honest, I rarely visited. Seeing all of the family portraits and pictures of Destiny almost caused me to pause. The hallway was lined with their family photos. Just seeing the evil grin on Dee's face in a pregnancy photo with Kendra reminded me to quicken my steps. I was so weak that my legs felt like heavy logs, making my steps heavy and uneven.

I reached the kitchen where the patio door was. I knew that was my only way out. I could see my freedom right in front of me. Right before I reached the patio door, I looked back to see if Dee was behind me. I didn't see or hear him. When I reached the patio door, I moved the vertical blinds back so that I could reach the lock. The blinds swung and hit against each other causing the noise to echo through the quiet house. I fumbled with the latch. I noticed that my hand was bleeding more and started to swell. The blood from my hand made the latch slippery.

I was able to undo the latch. I started to slide the door open when I felt a presence in the room. I turned to find a woman that I'd never seen before, approaching me quickly with a baseball bat raised high above her head. Before I could get the door open enough to slide through, the bat came crashing down across my back sending me down to the floor. My weak legs didn't hold me up against the force. I tried to crawl out the door, but she pulled me back by my hair and slammed me down on the floor. I tried to lift my feet to kick her, but I was too slow. She came down on me again with the bat, this time, I blocked it. The bat connecting with my forearm sent a cracking noise through the air as pain shot through my arm. I knew then my arm was broken. The last thing I remember was seeing this strange woman standing over me, swinging the bat as if she was trying to hit a home run for her team.

Linwood

alking out of the prison was like walking from the dead. I could feel the chains fall off. No longer was I to live like an animal, being told when and what to do. No longer was I told what to eat and when to eat it. I was physically locked up but my mind was always free. I read books every day; books that fed my brain. I had three goals when my feet hit the pavement; find my daughter, piss on Trey's grave and pay Kyle everything that he is owed. That day I called to tell Suga that I was coming home, I didn't expect to hear that my daughter was missing. After speaking with Santé, I thought back to Suga's visit. She didn't seem herself, even though I hadn't been in her life for many years, I still knew my daughter. She was definitely going through something, but I just couldn't put my finger on it. If she was anything like Teesa or myself, whatever it was, it was bad.

I walked straight ahead as I approached freedom. I was determined to not look back. I wanted to place prison so far back in my mind, that I would forget I was ever there. I was walking as far away from that place as possible.

"Linwood," I heard someone calling me.

I turned to find Kyle. He was slow jogging towards me in his fancy suit. I turned away and kept walking towards my destination.

"Hold up, man," Kyle said.

He caught up to me and stood directly in my path. I wanted to run his ass over, but I knew that wouldn't be the smart thing to do. He was going to get what he deserved.

"What?" I asked.

"Hold on. Where are you going? I came all the way out here to pick you up. I wanted to be sure you had a ride."

"I'm good."

I walked around him.

"Come on, man. What's the problem? I worked hard to get you out. This is how you repay me? Can I get a thank you or something?"

I stopped and turned to face him.

"Thank you for everything you ever did for me. Thank you for today. You're going to get everything you are owed and then you will see how much I appreciate you. Until then, stay the fuck out of my way."

The look on his face of pure fear and confusion was priceless. I could see his mind was racing trying to figure out what I meant by that. He's a smart man, I was sure he would figure it out sooner than later. From a distance, I heard a horn. I looked around. Running towards me was Santé. She reminded me so much of Suga. Right then, my heart ached. I didn't know where she was. I prayed that she left on her own and what I was told was only an assumption.

"Hey! It's me!" she shouted.

We embraced each other. I held her tightly.

"I'm so glad you're home. I know Suga is going…" she began to say.

I interrupted her and said, "Kyle, I have to get to my family. I'll talk to you later."

"Sure. Talk to you later," he responded.

Santé and I began to walk towards the car. She was still in my arms.

"I'm so sorry that you're coming home to all of this drama. When I came back down here to see Suga, I didn't know all of this happened. Unc, shit is looking real crazy," she said.

"What happened now?" I asked.

"He got a ransom call. They asking for a lot of money in the next couple days."

"That's not going to be a problem. I'm going to do whatever it takes to get my baby back. And the fool that thought he could pull a stunt like this is going to be dealt with."

"Ali is at Suga and Marlon's house helping him with everything. I know he got his back and will do whatever it takes to get her back to us."

"How's everything going with you and your boyfriend?"

"We're good. He's a really good man, I love him."

"Well since you love him I guess I'll have to let him live."

We both laughed.

As we drove down the highway, I rolled down my window and stuck my head out. I breathed in the fresh air. No words could describe how I felt at that very moment; to truly be free physically. I thanked God over and over for allowing me a second chance.

As we began to approach the city of Richmond I said, "Take me to my house."

"You want to go back to your old house?" she asked.

"Yes, that's still my house. Where did you think I was going? I know you ain't think I was coming home to nothing. You should know me better than that. If I don't have anything else in this world, I will have a roof over my head. I made sure of that. I really appreciate Redd, for taking care of the house all of these years."

"Are you sure you want to go back there. So much has happened in the house. It's like a bad omen. That house ain't nothing but bad luck if you ask me about it."

"No, it's not bad luck. I don't believe in that shit. True, some bad shit happened in that house, but it's mine. There was plenty of love in that house. It wasn't all bad."

"I don't know how you can want to go back there! Suga was almost killed and your grandson. Not to mention the devil himself, Trey, was killed there. Just saying this shit creeps me out. That house is not right. You can't pay me to go in there."

"I just asked you to drop me off. You don't have to go inside. That's my home. Where did you expect me to go when I got out? I know what happened there, I don't need you to remind me. I'm home now. I'm going to balance everything out. No more death is going to happen in my house. We're going to get back to love, life and good times. Teesa knew how to throw a good party. I'm trying to get back to that; good times."

With all the talk about death and Teesa, it sent me down memory lane. It pained me to hear or say her name, but I'd never let it show. I missed her so much. I blamed myself for everything and I had to live with that. All I knew to do was to come home and do right by my daughter and grandchild. First, I had to deal with a few things. I needed to pay my respects to Teesa and my disrespects to Trey.

As we entered my old neighborhood, I could tell that it had changed just like the rest of the world; life continued and the community grew. The main street leading to the neighborhood had a facelift with a few new businesses. I smiled as I admired the growth. Not that the neighborhood was in bad shape before I left, but it definitely came a long ways.

For the first time, I felt nervous. I fought off the anxiety I began to feel. I hadn't been home in so long that I had a sense of fear. I wasn't sure where the fear came from, but I summed it up to just nerves. As we drove closer, I recalled memories of Suga and her friends outside playing. When she saw my car turn the corner, she would run down the sidewalk towards my car. The sad part of it all was that I still saw her as my little girl. She was only sixteen when I went away. Although I knew she was a grown woman, I didn't see her as one.

"Wow, things has really changed around here. I barely recognize any of the houses. Which house is it?" Santé asked.

She drove slowly as we both looked for the house.

"There it is," I said. I pointed towards my home.

"It looks different," she said.

"The house was renovated. The entire inside should be completely different too."

"That's nice. That should make it somewhat easier to live in. You should sell that house."

"I told you there's nothing wrong with it. Look at it. I worked for this. This was my first piece of property. I would never sell it. I want to keep it in the family."

"I don't know why."

"So, you're not coming inside?"

"Hell no! You couldn't pay me to come in there. You know I'm superstitious, I pay attention to the signs."

"What signs?"

"You wouldn't know because you're not superstitious."

We pulled in front of the house, Santé left the car running and didn't show any signs that she was trying to see me inside.

"Thank you for picking me up," I said.

"No, problem. I'm just so glad that you are home!" she said.

She reached over and gave me a tight hug.

"Once I get settled in and get some wheels, I'll give you a call. I have a friend coming

over in a few hours to get me straight. Let Marlon know that I'm coming to see him tonight."

"I will. Call me if you need anything before then."

"I'm good, thank you."

Santé pulled off fast. I wasn't worried at all. Bad things

happened, but it was due to my karma. The worst things have happened to the people I love. The end of it was coming, but I had to save my child.

I walked quickly towards the house. Remembering that I didn't have a key, I walked

towards the backyard. I looked under the welcome mat and found the key. I'd asked Redd to

place a key there a week ago and I wasn't sure if he'd gotten around to it. Over the years, he'd became someone that I could trust and depend on; a friend.

I let myself in through the back door. Immediately, there was a beep from an alarm system. I didn't know the house had an alarm installed. I rushed inside in search of the panel. Inside, I didn't recognize the house. I felt as if I was in a stranger's home and not my own. It was completely different.

The alarm continued to beep. I rushed towards the living room. As soon as I found the panel on the wall, a loud siren began to sound off. I covered my ears as the deafening alarm blared.

"Shit!"

I looked for the phone, which wasn't on the end table in the living room where I remembered it. There wasn't an end table in the living room, there was all new furniture. I rushed back into the kitchen and just when I reached it, the cordless phone rang.

"Hello?" I answered.

I had one finger in my ear so that I could hear the caller.

"Who is this?" a voice asked from the other end of the phone.

"Who the fuck is this? You called my house!"

"This is Redd."

"This is Wood."

"That's all I needed to know. Hold a second."

As the alarm continued to sound, I anticipated the police running in at any moment. I strained my ears to hear what Redd was saying. I could hear him having another conversation. All of a sudden, the alarm stopped. My ears were still ringing when Redd came back on the line.

"Welcome home. How does it feel to be back on these streets?" Redd asked.

"It would feel much better if I wasn't coming home to this bullshit. We need to talk. It's about Suga."

"Look, I told you to give her some time. She'll come around. You have to understand that you've been out of her life for a long time. She's been through a lot and it's going to take some time for her to get used to you being around. I'll call and talk to her."

"Right now how she feels about me being back in her life is the least of my problems. You need to get over here as soon as you can."

"What's the problem?"

"I can't talk over this wire. We need to talk in person."

"Is something wrong with Suga?"

"We have a problem. Just get over here."

"I'm on my way."

After coming home to chaos with the security system that I didn't authorize to be installed, I was finally able to take it all in. The eerie thing was that I left with a family and came back to nothing. Even if I tried to redeem myself by going back to my wife, Marie, she'd already moved on with her life. She made sure to dog me out while I was down. After she'd found out about Teesa and Suga, she was hell-bent on making my life miserable because she could. She was the wife and she could pretty much destroy me. Other than taking my money, she slept with Kyle. They had a full out affair and didn't care to hide it. After she was done with him, she tossed him away and married her high school sweetheart. They moved out of the country due to him being in the military. I believe that she did that so that she never had to face me. She knew what type of a man I was, I wasn't going to let that go unpunished.

I loved Marie but I wasn't in love with her. She was unable to have children and that was something that I really wanted. I was young and married the first woman that made me feel like a man. She cooked for me, washed and ironed my clothes and she knew what to do in the bedroom. However, when I met Teesa, she made my heart feel something that it had never felt before. I fell in love with her. After I'd found out that she was having my child, that solidified my love. She gave me something that my wife was unable to give me; a child of my own.

My house was fully renovated and unrecognizable. Yet, it felt like home. I missed seeing Suga running around the house playing dress up. She wanted to be a diva just like her mother. Every day that I was down, I kicked myself. I wasn't there for her during a time that I was sure she needed me as a father. She was sixteen and becoming a woman. It was my job to show her what a man was supposed to be.

After I ended the call with Redd, I heard a hard knock at the front door. I looked towards the opened back door, expecting police to storm the door pointing guns in my face. I knew not to move so I just waited. There was another loud knock. I walked to the back door and looked out. I didn't see anyone. I closed and locked it. I went to the front door to answer it.

"Who is it?" I asked.

"It's me!" a sexy voice said.

I opened the door to find Mona standing on my front porch. She and I had been pen pals for three years. She held me down during that time. She didn't miss a letter or a visit. I loved her for that. The true test was if she was going to be there once I got out. So far, she passed the test. Mona was a gorgeous, thick boned girl with a beautiful smile and great personality. Most of all she was intelligent. She'd always hit me with large words that I'd have to look up in a dictionary and use on her when I could. She was the type of woman that encouraged her man and helped you get to where you wanted to be in your life. We'd met through one of my old cellmates, Matt. He'd received a letter from his wife with a photo of her with three other women. I noticed Mona's bright smile, she seemed so full of life. I was instantly attracted to her. Looking at her picture made me smile. After convincing Matt to write his wife asking about the girl with the beautiful smile, it wasn't long before I started receiving letters from her. We started writing each other almost every week. Then she started accepting my calls and visiting.

"Hey, baby! You're home!" she said.

She leaped into my arms and laid a kiss on me that immediately made my dick hard.

When she finally let me come up for air I said, "Damn, woman you sure know how to welcome a man home."

"Do you know how long I've waited for this? It's been three years. I can't believe you're home."

"It's been longer for me. I haven't been with a woman in a very long time. So be gentle."

"Oh, baby. You are in for a treat. I told you I was going to be here when you came home and I meant it. I love you, Linwood."

She turned around and pointed to her bags.

"Staying for a while?" I asked. She had grocery bags and a suitcase.

"Don't play with me, Wood. You said you wanted me to stay for a couple of days. Don't you remember? You said that in your letter. Is there a problem?" she asked.

"No problem. It's just that something came up and I probably won't be here as much I planned. You know that I would have you here every day if I could. It's been a very long time since I had a woman."

"That's okay. I'll be here. Handle your business."

That put a smile on my face. I didn't want her to expect me to be laid up with her for the next couple of days when I had to find Suga.

"Why don't you go upstairs and get ready for me. I'll be right behind you."

"Don't make me wait too long. I've waited long enough for this."

I watched her walk away. It took everything in me not to fuck her where she stood, but I had to get to my money.

I waited a few minutes before going to the attic. I clearly instructed Redd not to touch the attic. It was clear when I got upstairs that someone was in the attic because the lock was removed from the attic door.

"Fuck!"

I rushed to pull down the ladder. I rushed up the ladder and into the attic. I coughed immediately as dust entered my lungs. The attic was cluttered with boxes and old furniture. I looked around for my plastic tubs. I moved boxes and furniture in search of my money. They weren't there. My money and valuables were gone. Without Suga, I couldn't get the money from the bank and now more money was gone. I had to get it all back or go back to what I knew best.

Suga

I rolled over to my sleeping baby boy, Junior. He was dressed in all white. It appeared to be the very christening outfit that his grandmother had purchased for him. I thought about my mother. Tears fell from my eyes as I thought about how much Junior was going to miss with her not being around. He had Marlon's mother, but he wouldn't have mine in his life. I wept for my mother. She had gone through so much in her life, especially sacrificing herself for me.

My baby lay there so calmly. He was such a happy baby. He kicked his legs and smiled at me. I wiped my tears and kissed my baby, and then my baby was gone. I sat up and called out to him. There was nowhere to search for him. I was in a white space with nothing around me. I couldn't see anything but white. When I turned around, there was Trey, holding Junior in his arms. He had a sadistic look on his face, just the way I remembered it before he tried to kill me.

"Give me back my baby!" I yelled.

I moved towards him and then he disappeared. I searched around and saw nothing.

"Trey! Where are you? Please don't hurt my baby!"

I woke up in a cold sweat. It didn't take me long to remember where I was except that I wasn't in the same room that I'd been in. I wasn't in the basement. I was in a bedroom. I tried to sit up, but was forced back down by a pain and heaviness in my head.

"I wouldn't do that if I were you," a woman said.

I turned to the right of me to find a woman sitting by the bed, reading a book. She looked faintly familiar. Then I realized she was the woman that I was fighting with when I tried to escape.

She sat her book down and looked at me with concern. She came closer to me and tried to touch my head. I backed away from her.

"Look at you. You're bleeding through your dressing again. I didn't mean to hit you so hard with that bat. When you break into someone's home, you can get hurt or even killed," she said.

"I didn't break in! Dee had me hostage down in that basement!" I said.

"No, he didn't! He said he caught you breaking into the basement and you attacked him down there. Look at you. You're filthy. Are you a junkie or what? That's what you look like."

I realized that Dee planted a seed in her head. Instead of arguing with her, I had to reason with her if I wanted to convince her otherwise.

"Who are you?" I asked.

"Don't worry about who I am. Who are you?" she asked.

The woman sat on the side of the bed with a first aid kit. I was completely aware of my injuries. I remember her hitting me with a bat, breaking my arm. I felt my head and it was bandaged. My arm was swollen and resting on a pillow. I worried that there could be serious issues considering the fact that I was still recovering from my previous injuries, a head injury being one. I'd already had a scar on my forehead and didn't need another.

"Let me look at it," she said. She moved my hand away gently.

She carefully pulled back the bandages. It stuck to my scalp and she sprayed something on it to remove it more easily. Once removed, I saw that the bandages were bloody. I tried to touch my head and she stopped me.

"No, don't touch it with your dirty hands, you'll infect it," she said.

We locked eyes. I pleaded with her with my eyes, hoping she would have some compassion for me.

"How bad is it?" I asked.

"It's a gash that may need some stitches. I cleaned it and put a bandage on it. You should be fine until you leave," she said.

"He's letting me leave?"

"Yes. Why wouldn't he? You're lucky he didn't call the police on you. He wants you to stay here so he can help you. We see that you have a problem."

"What the fuck are you talking about? I don't have a

problem! Dee is the problem. He is crazy! He kidnapped me from my home and brought me here. He's been holding me against my will down in that basement. He is lying to you so that you don't spoil his plan."

"What plan? What are you talking about? I've been here all day with him and no one else was here. Dee isn't like that. I know he doesn't know you. Now stop telling your lies!"

"My name is Suga Cole. My husband is Marlon Cole. We own the Cole's Jewelry stores. I have a newborn son named after his father. Dee and my husband are best friends. Kendra, Dee's wife, was my best friend. Dee has gone ballistic. He has always been jealous of my husband. This time, he has gone too far. He's going to kill me if I don't get out of here!"

"Why would he kidnap you? Look at you. You're all dirty and stinky. You're nothing more than a junkie prostitute like he said. You came here to steal so you can get your next fix. I know your kind. Look at your dirty ass."

My head was hurting so badly that I wanted to give up the fight. I knew that I had to appeal to her. I needed her to help me get out of there. I decided to lower my voice in order to fight off a banging headache.

"I own any designer you can name. I look like this only because I've been down in that basement. Please help me! I need to get back to my husband and my son. They need me. If you don't help me, he's going to kill me," I said.

She backed away from me.

"I don't believe you," she said.

"You can Google my store, Cole's Jewelry. You will find a

picture of my husband and me. If I'm right, will you please call him and tell him where I am?"

She took a moment to think about it. I knew this was my last chance to convince her that I wasn't who Dee said I was.

"Okay. If you're lying then you don't have to worry about me helping you at all."

I nodded my head and tears began to stream down my face as I thought about being back home safe with my family. At that moment, I realized what a blessing Marlon was to me and how much he meant to me. I loved that man. I loved my son. I couldn't imagine living without either one of them. The very thing that I fought against having was the very thing that could keep me alive.

"What is your name?" I asked.

"My name is Lex."

She gave me a slight smile. I watched her pull out her cell phone from her pocket and began to type. I waited quietly although I wanted to say more. I knew that we didn't have much time. Dee wasn't going to leave her alone with me too long. I watched as she looked at me then back at her phone a few times. I knew she saw that it was me.

"Oh my, God! It is you! Why? Why are you here?" she asked.

"I told you! Now call my husband, please. Hurry before he gets back!"

I watched her fumble with her phone.

"I don't want to have anything to do with this. I don't know what the fuck is going on here," she said.

"It's too late for that. You are involved now. Call my husband and I'll make sure you get out of this," I said.

"What's his number? Hurry up before he gets back."

"His number is eight..."

Just before I could finish giving her Marlon's number, Dee slowly opened the door. I quickly closed my eyes and pretended to be asleep. I prayed that Lex would stay calm and think fast.

"Is she still asleep?" Dee asked.

"Yes, she hasn't woke up yet. Do you think she's okay?" Lex asked.

"I thought I heard voices in here," he said.

"You did, mine. I was talking to my sister. I got bored sitting in here watching her sleep."

"You didn't say anything about this, did you?"

"Of course not."

"I knew I could trust you."

"I told you that. I got you, baby."

"There's pizza downstairs. Help yourself. I know you need a break. I took a little longer than I was supposed to, sorry."

"Baby, it's not a problem. I can sit up here a little longer if you want me to. You go ahead and eat. I got this."

There was a pause in their conversation.

"I thought you said you were getting bored in here watching her?" he asked.

"I was, but I know you're tired," she said.

There was another pause.

"I got it. Go downstairs."

"Okay, baby."

I laid as still as I could. My heart was beating so fast that I swore they could hear it. I tried to keep my breathing steady and tried not to move. I couldn't let him take me back to the basement. Somehow, I knew that if I was to go back to the basement, I wasn't going to come back out alive. I waited and listened to see if Lex was going to convince him to let her stay. I needed to tell her Marlon's phone number.

"Go ahead. I'll be down in a minute," he said.

"Well, okay. Don't keep me waiting," she said.

I heard them kiss and a moment later, the door closed.

I assumed Lex left the room and I was left alone with Dee. I was scared to be alone with him. I didn't know when he was going to try to kill me. After stabbing him, I was sure he was going to seek revenge on me. As my mind began to race, I felt someone sit down beside me on the bed. I waited to hear the voice of Dee or Lex. I could feel my body began to shake in fear.

"You little bitch. I know you can hear me. If you think you're going to get out of this alive, you're wrong. I'm going to get my money and then kill you. If it wasn't for you, Kendra might still be alive. You left my baby to die in that hospital. You could've made her fight harder for me and Destiny, but you didn't," he said.

I wanted to jump up and smack the monkey shit out of his crazy ass. This was the second time that he blamed me for Kendra's death. Dee was so far gone that I almost thought there was no way he would come back from this. He needed help and he needed it fast. I had no idea that he was mourning Kendra the way that he was.

"Wake up!" he said.

I didn't move. I refused to acknowledge him.

"I said, wake up!" he said. This time, he slapped me across my face.

I grabbed my face and tried to sit up to defend myself. He grabbed both of my arms and pinned me down. I screamed out in agony as my broken arm twisted.

"Get off of me! Help!" I yelled.

I almost called out to Lex, but quickly remembered that I wasn't supposed to know her name.

"Shut up before I snap your little neck. Then you will be dead before I can have you call to prove that you're still alive," he said.

I calmed down at the thought of possibly getting the chance to talk to Marlon.

"I hate you! I can't believe you have stooped to such low levels. Extortion and kidnapping, really? You want someone to blame for Kendra's death. Blame yourself. You were supposed to protect her. You should've been the one to die that night, not her," I said.

He stood to his feet and peered down at me. Then he paced the floor beside the bed.

"I did protect her. I did all I could to protect my house. He came into my house! He tried to take me out in my house! Destiny could've been here. My family could've been here," he said.

I watched him pound his chest like King Kong as he spoke those words. I shifted my body towards the opposite side of the bed closest to the door and readied myself for an escape. He pulled a set of handcuffs out of his back pocket. I knew that if he put me in handcuffs I wouldn't be able to escape.

"What are those for?" I asked calmly.

He looked at me as if I had two heads and said, "It's for you, stupid."

"I can't even stand on my own two feet. My hip is hurting," I said. "You know my arm is broken."

"Yeah, right. I just saw you running faster than Flo Jo out of that basement. I know you can walk."

"That was my adrenaline. Trust me I paid for it."

"Trust you? Not in this lifetime."

He grabbed my arm so quick that I didn't have a chance to react. He cuffed me to the metal headboard. When he was standing over me I caught a glimpse of a gun tucked in the small of his back. At that moment, I decided not to piss him off too much. I was terrified of guns. The day Trey pointed that gun in my face was the first and last time that I prayed I would ever have that happen to me again. Although he didn't shoot me, he did enough damage by pistol whooping me.

"Now I'm going to call Marlon and I want you to tell him that you are alive and well. If you say anything to tip him off about me or where you are I'm going to kill you," he said.

He pulled out the gun that I prayed he wouldn't use on me and held it down by his side.

"I don't care what you do to me. I'm not going to let you take our hard earned money when you plan on killing me anyway. Fuck you!" I said.

I was scared shitless. But I was trying to buy some time to think about what I could say to tip Marlon off without letting Dee know. I knew that I didn't have much longer before it was time to get rid of me. There was no way Dee was going to let me go. I could see the thirst for blood and revenge in his eyes.

"What if I take a little visit to see your son at his grandmother's house?" he said.

"Okay, I'll do it you crazy bastard! How could you threaten a child? You have a daughter too," I said.

"Do what I say and then I won't hurt your son."

I stared at him in disbelief that he would threaten a harmless child and to know that Marlon loved this monster like a brother made me sick. When Marlon finds out that Dee was behind this he was going to be devastated.

"I'm going to call him. When I give you the phone, talk to him. Tell him what he needs to hear. But if you say anything about me I'm going to blow your head off. And don't think I won't do it. I'll kill that bitch downstairs too."

"No! I'm not going to do it. I don't care what you do to me!" I spit in his direction.

"You may not care what I'll do to you, but you will care what will happen to Junior."

At that moment, I vomited all over myself.

"Oh, so you care about the little bastard." He let out a loud laugh. "You actually care about someone other than yourself. Too bad for Kendra that you finally figured out that other people matter."

"You'll stoop so low to threaten a defenseless child? He hasn't done anything to you. How could you hurt a child? You're really sick," I said through my tears.

"I'm making this call and you better make it sound convincing or else."

"How could you do this to him? He has been there for you and your family your entire lives. He loves you like a brother and you repay him like this?"

"Repay him? Marlon owes me more than he can ever repay me! I was the one in these streets putting in work while he was off in college trying to play the good ole boy, fooling his parents and everyone around him that he changed. He was a dope boy! I helped build those businesses with my blood, sweat and tears. He thought that feeding me the scraps off his table was going to keep me satisfied while he's living like a king. He owes me. How is he going to repay me?"

"Don't do this, Dee. It's not too late for you to turn this around. Just let me go. I'll keep with the story that I was leaving him and that I changed my mind. I'm sure you didn't mean for all of this to happen like this. Why would you have me tell him that I was leaving him if you planned to extort him for money? I can go back as if I changed my mind. I could do it, I know I can. Marlon would forgive me and things would go back as they were," I pleaded with him.

He let out a laugh that sent chills through my body.

"You know what, you're right. I didn't plan for things to turn out like this. I was going to kill you and watch him suffer. Then I was going to rob and kill him the way I should've killed him the night I caught him fucking my wife! That was the plan, you should've been dead. Then I came up with the idea of getting more money and the best way to do that was to use you. So yeah, my plans changed."

There was a knock on the door.

"If you say a word I'll put one in the both of you. Do you understand?" he whispered.

I didn't answer him.

"Come in," he said.

Lex entered the room with a plate and bottled water.

"I wanted to bring you something to eat," she said.

She looked at me in surprise as if she'd never seen me before.

"Oh, look. The little thief is awake," she said. "Looks like she needs this more than you do," she said.

Before he could protest, she quickly handed me the plate. She was taken back when she saw my handcuffed arm.

"Why did you cuff her? How is she going to eat? I think her other arm is broken," she asked.

"She tried to fight me and run away. I didn't know what else to do," he said.

I could tell that Lex was becoming a believer. If she had any doubt that Dee was really up to no good, she knew then. He uncuffed me.

I picked up the pizza with my free hand and began to eat it. I swallowed the pizza in record time and was back to planning my escape.

"How long is she supposed to be here like this? This isn't making any sense," Lex said.

"Mind your damn business. If you don't like what's going on then maybe you should leave," he said.

Lex looked at me and I looked at her. I prayed that she wouldn't allow him to make her leave. I needed her there.

"No, this is your house. Do what you want," she said.

She walked out of the room, but left the door open. I looked at Dee who was starting to sweat. He kept looking towards the door and then turned his attention on me.

"Now let's get this done. I'm going to call Marlon and you're going to talk to him. Don't tell him who I am or where you are. Tell him to pay up or you're going to die. It's your job to convince him to pay or you know what the consequences are. I'm going to put you on speakerphone so don't be stupid. You got it?" he asked.

I didn't answer him. He dialed a number and placed the call on speakerphone. As the phone rang, I anticipated hearing Marlon's voice. I didn't wait long before I heard his voice. Dee nodded towards me to speak.

"Marlon," I said.

"Suga? Baby is this you?" he asked.

I immediately began to cry at the sound of his voice.

"Yes, it's me. Baby, I don't have much time. I was told to tell you to pay the ransom or he'll kill me," I said.

Dee gave me a daring look as if I was saying too much.

"Who the fuck did this? Tell me baby. Tell me where to find you, please?" Marlon asked.

"I can't tell you that or he'll kill me. Marlon, do whatever it takes to find me. Hurry…" I began to say.

As Dee removed the phone from my ear, I could still hear Marlon talking.

"I love you!" I called out before Dee could hang up the phone.

"Good job. Tomorrow all of this will be over," Dee said.

He pulled out a bag of pills and removed one from the bag.

"No! I'm not going to take it!" I screamed.

"Yes, you will. By force or choice, it's up to you. Once I get my money, we're going to leave this city. Destiny and I deserve to live the good life and we will," he said.

"You don't deserve to have Destiny. Kendra would've never gone along with this."

"Don't talk to me about my wife! You weren't a friend to her. She was a better friend to you than you were to her. Don't say her name out of your mouth again!"

"You're so sick! I hate you!"

"I hate you more. Now, get the water bottle and take this pill. I don't want any more shit out of you."

I wiped my tears with my free hand as I replayed the conversation I had with Marlon. I missed him so much. I could hear the fear in his voice. I could only imagine what he was going through. I wondered if he reported me missing and if the police were out there looking for me. I hoped so. Lex was my only hope. I knew she was going to do the right thing. I had to believe that. If not, then my only chance of being found was gone because I failed to tell Marlon where I was in that phone call. Doing that, I risked the safety of my son. I prayed that Lex would save me.

He continued to hold me at gunpoint and forced me to drink the water and take the pill. As he waited for the pill to take effect, I cried as I hung on to the sound of Marlon's determined voice and my son. I was beginning to think that it was over for me as I saw my great escape plan fade away with my consciousness.

CHAPTER 16

Santé

After spending some time with my family and trying not to show the stress that I was under, I headed back to the hotel with Ali. Ali didn't want me to stay in the house with Marlon alone after the ransom call so I checked us into a hotel. The hotel was swank and known as one of the historic hotels in the city. Out of the times that I'd come down to visit, this was the time that every soul wanted to ask me where was Suga. I tried to avoid the question by simply saying, "She's doing great and so is the little one." It wasn't like she visited with my side of the family often, but they loved her.

Everyone had known that she'd just given birth to her first child and they were happy for her. Now that Linwood was home, they were more concerned about her relationship with him. My mom was very upset that I didn't bring Linwood over to see them as soon as he came home, but I assured them that he was going to visit them the next day. As much as I wanted to let the family know what was going on and could use their support, I knew that it would complicate things further. I needed to sit back and pray that between Ali, Linwood and Marlon, they would find her.

I was exhausted by the time I'd arrived at the hotel. Ali had the champagne on chill and our dinner already ordered. I wanted to take a shower and relax, but we had business to discuss. With Suga's disappearance, I didn't know where our plans stood. I knew that Ali wanted to discuss business, but I was starting to have a change of heart.

"Hey, baby," I said.

Ali greeted me with a hug and kiss.

"Hey," he replied.

"I'm so exhausted. I just want to shower and lay down."

"You know we have business to discuss first."

"I know, but can't it wait until tomorrow."

"No, it can't. We were supposed to execute our plan tomorrow. This was your hit, you told me that you had this all planned and figured out. We were supposed to rob your cousin's store. So now, what are we going to do?"

I sighed.

"It seemed like a good idea at first. I knew that they had insurance and would see that money back. Now, with everything that has happened, I feel bad about this. Suga has gone through hell and back since I came up with that plan. Now look, she's been abducted. Like, this shit is crazy!" I said.

"So, you don't want to go through with this? Remember this was your plan."

"I know, but I don't think it's a good idea now. Too much has changed."

"Did Marlon call the police yet?"

"No, I don't think so. I think he's going to call them tomorrow."

"Okay. That gives us a chance to get in, take what we need, and get out."

"No! I can't do this right now. My Uncle Linwood is home. Do you know what he would do to you if he finds out about this? You don't know him."

"No one is going to know as long as you follow my plan. Trust me."

Ali began to rub on my thighs and kiss me deeply. He stopped suddenly.

"Hold on. I know just what you need."

I knew where he was going and why. As much as I wanted to tell him no, I wanted to say yes. I was controlled by a demon; one that I'd kept hidden. I fought that demon every day and sometimes I won and others I lost the fight.

Ali returned waving a plastic bag. A smile almost crept across my face anticipating what was to come. Ali never used drugs that I could tell. But he didn't seem to have a problem offering me drugs when he wanted to have his way. In the beginning, he started complaining that I didn't listen to him and that I didn't show him respect. He swore to never put his hands on me although he'd come close to it a few times. Shortly after that, he offered me some cocaine.

I knew that cocaine wasn't something that I needed to add to my life. I never was one to do drugs. My choice was alcohol.

I refused him over and over again. I knew it was a way for him to control me and I was determined not to let that happen.

One night, after partying with Queenie, I came in drunk and later than Ali would've like for me to return home. We argued about it, but I was too drunk to stay in the fight. I remember going to bed and Ali following me. That was the first time I took a hit of cocaine. He assured me that he wouldn't let me develop a habit. I wondered why he offered me drugs when he said that he loved me.

"I know just what you need when you get like this," he said. He waved the plastic bag in my face.

"No, thank you," I forced myself to say.

I began to walk towards the bathroom. Ali pulled me by my arm to face him.

"I can't have you out of control like this. I can't have you against me in this plan, it won't work without you," he said.

He squeezed my arm. I looked down at the grip that he had on my arm.

"Really? Are you going to put your hands on me now?" I asked.

"Never, but you're going to listen to me."

"I don't want any of your drugs. Do you want to turn me out now?"

"Of course not. I will never let you develop a habit."

"Of course not," I said mockingly. "You just want to control me."

He let me go. I rubbed my aching arm.

"I guess I'll flush this since you don't want it. I only had it for you," he said.

Ali crumpled the bag in his fist and headed toward the bathroom. I watched him.

I held myself back from running behind him. I wanted it and my body craved it. I sat on the edge of the bed and rocked back and forth as I fought the urge to stop him.

A few seconds later, I heard the toilet flush. I rushed into the bathroom where I found Ali lifting the hotel key card with a corner of cocaine up to his nose.

"What… What are you doing?" I asked in shock.
"I knew you couldn't resist. I saved some for you too," he said. He added more coke to the key card and offered it to me.

I accepted his offer. Together we took the ride. This was a first and I liked it. I'd never seen Ali take drugs. Just like every other time, I regretted my actions but fought with the feeling of euphoria. I didn't want to become a junkie or dependent upon a drug. I figured as long as I didn't let it consume me and I stayed on top of my game, I would be fine. Now that Ali was enjoying the ride with me, I had to be especially careful. Neither of us could afford to lose ourselves.

I held my head back and squeezed the tip of my nose. I closed my eyes as I waited. Ali lifted me up onto the counter; he slid up my skirt and removed my panties. I leaned back until I rested against the large mirror behind me. Ali began to plant kisses between my inner thighs. I wanted him so badly. He worked his way to my moist center and began to please me with his wet, warm tongue. My back arched as he pushed his tongue further inside of me. I moaned with pleasure as he moved his mouth up my stomach and to my breast. I felt his hardness pressing against my thighs. I grabbed his manhood and guided him inside. He filled me up as we both gasped. He lifted me from the counter and I wrapped my legs around his hard muscular body. He held me tightly, cupping my ass. We kissed as he bounced me up and down on him. When it was over we took a hot shower together.

"That was awesome," I said.

"I know it. I hope that helped you get your mind right," he said.

"I don't want to do this, but I am. I don't want anything to go wrong and I don't want my cousin hurt behind this," I said.

"How is she not going to be hurt? Her place of business is going to be robbed. No matter how much insurance they have, they're going to take a loss. Stop worrying and focus on the plan. If things go wrong, we could be doing a long ass bid," he said.

"That's what I'm afraid of…"

"The family is coming over in the morning to go over the final details and get the ball rolling on this. We don't have much time."

I didn't respond to him. I just stepped out of the shower and prayed that everything went as planned. In my gut, I felt that something was going to go wrong. Things were off and Suga's situation was the first sign of that.

Marlon

I had to get out of the house. The walls felt as if they were closing in on me. I'd just spoken to Suga. The woman on the other end of the phone was terrified. It killed me to hear the fear in her voice. She was unable to tell me who took her or where she was being held. The entire time all I could imagine was somebody standing over her, threatening her with a weapon if she didn't say the right thing.

Dee couldn't get to my house fast enough. I had to fill him in on everything that transpired since he'd been out looking for Suga. I thought about getting the police involved at this point because I didn't have any experience dealing with this type of situation. It seemed as easy as paying the ransom in exchange for Suga, but I knew that it wasn't going to be that simple.

My energy was low because I hadn't been eating. I didn't have an appetite at all, but knew that I would need energy just in case something went down. I went into the kitchen to grab a piece of fruit. While reaching for an apple, I saw the notebook that Suga used to write her letter to me. Beside it was the letter. I picked it up and read it again. I read it as if I would be able to decode who took her and why. I felt weak in the situation not knowing what to do. I looked at the notebook she tore the paper from. I thought maybe she wrote more and something urged me to pick it up. At first glance, it didn't appear to be anything written at all. Then I looked more closely. Very lightly, the word *'Help me, Dee'* was written on the paper. It wasn't in Suga's handwriting at all. It didn't look anything like the writing from her letter. I didn't know what that meant.

Was she trying to send me a message?

A heavy knock on the front door broke my train of thought. I yanked my front door open to find a man that I've never seen before. He looked vaguely familiar.

"Can I help you?" I asked.

"Are you Marlon?" the man asked.

"Who wants to know?"

"I'm Linwood, Suga's father. Can I come in?"

I'd seen pictures of him and had no doubt in my mind that the man standing in front of me was Linwood. He was just older. I let my guard down and invited him inside.

"Yes, sure. Come in."

Linwood walked in and instantly I felt his presence. He had a very strong presence when he entered.

"How are you?" he asked. He extended his hand and I accepted. I felt some of the weight lift off of my shoulders knowing that another person that loved Suga just as much as I did was there.

"Mr. White, I could be better. I wish we were meeting under much better circumstances. I have to tell you what's going on with Suga."

"I already know, Santé told me that someone took my daughter and you needed help finding her. Do you know anything about what happened to Suga?"

"All I know is that I'm getting calls now demanding money for her return. I was able to talk to her on this last call and I can tell my baby is fucked up. Another thing, her abductors had her write a letter as if she was leaving me. Now they are calling for money. That doesn't make sense at all."

"Sounds like they had a change of heart and good thing they did. They might've had plans to just kill her. The letter was to keep you from looking for her and to cause you pain. This is personal."

"Shit is real out here! They want to bring the beast out! I left the streets a long time ago for Suga. I'm trying not to lose it out here! They fucked with my heart."

"I know how you're feeling. She's my daughter. I got you."

"Everyone seems to be saying that now."

"Who are these people? No one is going to go harder than those that truly love her. That's me and you. Any other help we get is good, but we are the ones that are going to go to hell and back for her."

Before I could explain, a horn blared from outside. It was Dee with his music blasting.

"Where is my grandson?" he asked.

"He's safe. I don't have much time to find her before the exchange. I'm on my way out with my boy, Dee. You're more than welcome to come with us, but I have to go."

"You go ahead. Take down my number and call me as soon as you hear something." He reached into his jacket pocket and pulled out a gold pen.

I looked around for something to write with and handed him the notebook. I watched him write.

"What's this?" he asked.

"What?" I asked.

He turned the paper around so that I could see it. The horn blared again.

"That's what I was trying to figure out when you arrived. This is the same notebook that Suga used to write her letter. This was the next page with my boy Dee's name on it."

I watched Linwood's face turn almost white.

"She was trying to tell you who did this. That's my girl!" he said.

"Do you think she wrote this without being seen? I'm sure they were watching her the entire time."

"Is that who's outside now?"

I began to pace back and forth. Dee was looking more and more guilty.

"Yes, I've been back and forth with this. I don't want to believe that fool would do that to me! After all I've done for him! I'm going to kill him!" I said.

I pulled my gun out the small of my back and headed towards the door.

"No, son. Wait! We have to find Suga. Killing him now

isn't going to get us any closer to her with him dead. We have to play him close. It's going to be hard, but you have to keep your cool if you want to bring her home."

I tried to keep it together. My blood boiled in my veins. I wanted to kill Dee so bad I could see him lying dead in front of me.

"Stay calm Marlon. You now have the upper hand on him. If he has her, he's going to lead us right to her," he said.

"How can I be calm? He got my wife! He's trying to use her to get to my money. That

bitch is going to pay! Fuck that!" I shouted.

"Come on, son. Keep your head or we'll never get her back. We need him alive. Now

go ahead and do whatever y'all already had planned."

I shook my head in disbelief. I couldn't believe Dee would bite the hand that fed him. We were brothers.

"You can do this. You have my number. You're not in any danger as long as he believes you're going to pay up. Let him believe that. Don't let your anger cause you to lose our only link to finding my daughter."

I tried to calm down. I'd seen Suga do these breathing exercises where she inhales and exhales until she is calm. I thought about my son and how important it was for him to have his mother.

"Okay. I got this. But I swear on everything I love I'm going to be the one to put a bullet through his head."

Just then, Dee walked into the house. With his normal arrogance, he walked in as if he lived there. I recognized this as a form disrespect now that I really knew how he felt about me. He'd done this numerous times and each time Suga spoke on it. I guess I was the only one blind to it.

"What's taking you so long?" he asked.

I stared him down as I gripped my gun tighter. Linwood didn't say a word. He just looked at Dee too.

"Did I interrupt something? You good, man?" Dee asked. He stared Linwood down.

Things were starting to get intense.

Linwood held out his hand and said, "I'm Linwood, Suga's father. Marlon was telling me that my daughter wasn't here. I was just leaving."

Dee went to shake his hand and pulled his hand back in pain. He grabbed his shoulder.

"What's wrong with you?" I asked.

"Just my shoulder. It's been giving me hell lately," Dee said.

"Well, tell Suga to call me when she gets in," Linwood said. He walked towards the door and stopped. He turned back and said, "I didn't get your name."

"I'm Dee. A friend of the family," Dee said.

"A friend of the family. In this family we have to be careful who we call our friends," Linwood said. "I'm sure I'll be seeing you again." Linwood walked out the door.

"Who the fuck do he think he is? Where the fuck did he come from?" Dee asked.

"Don't worry about him," I said.

"Man, what's up with you? You mad or some shit?" Dee asked.

"What the fuck you think?" I said.

"Come on, man. We got to get out of here. We have to go see Theo," he said.

SNOOK

I took in a deep breath and followed him out the door.

Theo was a neighborhood dealer when I was coming up. He was the flashy type with the latest shoes, clothes, and gold jewelry. I wanted to be just like him. One day, Theo was robbed and shot five times. He survived and came back stronger. He left the corner and started a business. He owned a tire and rim shop, but sold more than that. He paid for protection and been running his business for years untouched.

As we rode in his car, Dee did most of the talking. He was talking about leaving Richmond and starting over somewhere else. I knew that he planned to take my money and buy him a new life. The thought of my son was the only thing that kept me off his ass. I just set back and let him talk himself into his grave.

"We're about to pull up at Theo's shop. You know we can't take our guns in there," Dee said.

I knew that we couldn't take guns inside the shop because Theo didn't trust anyone; that I didn't like. I needed my gun as long as the devil was by my side.

"Here, put it in here," Dee said.

Dee opened his glove compartment and then pressed another button where another hidden compartment opened. I still had my gun in my hand, but reluctantly placed it in the compartment.

"Man, you good? You haven't said a word since we left your house. I know you all fucked up behind this, but you gotta get your mind right. They don't really fuck with us like that," he said.

"I'm good. I've just been doing some thinking, that's all.

Let's get this shit over with and see what information he has," I said.

"That's what I'm talking about. We got to get to the bottom of this bullshit. If we take any longer, you're going to have to pay the money. It don't seem to be a word on the streets about her. I don't know, but if Theo information isn't good, we're going to have to figure out how to get this money up," Dee said.

"We? You putting up?"

"I mean, you. You know I don't have the paper like that."

"You sound stupid! With all that "we" shit! We don't have a wife that's been taken and could die if I don't come up off some major paper!" I shouted.

I didn't wait for Dee's response. I got out the car as fast as I could before I ruined any chance of using him to get to Suga. Dee was right behind me. I could feel the heat on my back from the look he was giving me.

When we approached the shop, Luck was standing at the front door. We greeted each other with a normal head nod. Luck patted us both down and led us to the back of the tire and rim shop. Half way to the back office, he let us go the rest of the way alone.

We found Theo seated at his desk with a strange look on his face. His head was tilted back. We walked into his office.

"What's up, Theo," I said.

Theo sat up quickly and began to fumble with his pants.

"Oh, what's up?" Theo said.

"Damn it. You made me hit my head," a young woman said.

She rubbed the top of her head and stood to her feet. She had on a tight dress and platform heels. The dark bags around her eyes made it hard to tell how old she was. She was young knowing Theo.

"I don't have much time," I said.

"I understand under the circumstances. Take a seat," Theo said. He looked over at the young woman and said, "What are you waiting for? Get out of here! I have business to handle!"

"You didn't pay me," she said.

"You didn't finish," Theo said.

"Don't try to play me like that!" she shouted.

"Come back in ten minutes," Theo said.

The girl smiled and said, "Okay, then. I'll be back in ten minutes."

The girl left the office and closed the door behind her.

"Take a seat," Theo said.

I looked around the cluttered office. The sofa looked like he found it on the side of the road. Dee sneezed twice since we'd been in the room because the dust was so thick, making it hard to breathe.

"I'll stand," I said.

"Cool. Well, I may have information that could help you with your situation," Theo said.

"That's why I'm here," I said.

"Look, Theo, we don't have all day. What's up?" Dee interjected.

"I heard you have a little situation with your wife," Theo said.

"What situation is that?" I asked.

"Dee has been running around town asking questions about your wife. I figured she must be in some kind of trouble or something. Especially, after everything that happened recently," Theo said.

I didn't comment. I knew he was talking about what happened with Trey. There were many rumors about what happened that day. No thanks to the news media for reporting half-truths and never following up with the facts.

"I heard your wife, Suga, was involved in Trey's death. I'm not sure about the details, but his people seem to think she did. I heard that his people want blood for his murder," Theo said.

"He tried to kill my wife and he killed her mother. He went there to rob the place and came up with nothing. He could've killed my son!" I said.

"Hold up! Don't shoot the messenger. I'm just telling you what I know. His people isn't happy with your family right now. Maybe, just maybe all of this could be linked. I just wanted to let you know. Do with it what you please," Theo said.

"So, why are you telling me this?" I asked.

I knew that this information didn't come without a price.

"The same people that may have touched your house, robbed one of my delivery trucks. Let's say I had more than tire and rims on that truck. They set me back in a major way. The way I see it, they would see me coming a mile away. But you, they don't know about that silent killer you have behind you. They think you're some square with money. They're too young to know about you from the streets. They don't respect you," Theo said.

"I talked to one of those young boys before and I heard they were running around making threats against the family. We have an understanding. I don't think they had anything to do with this. If they did, I know where to find them," Dee said.

"Good, then both of our problems would be solved," Theo said. He smiled showing his gold fronts.

I walked out the office, but Dee stayed behind for a few minutes. Just as I approached the car, my phone rang.

"Hello?"

"Mr. Cole, this is Francis. I'm at the store. There's a woman here that wants to speak with you. She said she has some information about Suga," she said.

"Who is she?" I asked.

"She wouldn't give me her name. Mr. Cole, is everything all right?" Francis whispered into the phone.

"Yes, all is well. You can put her on the phone," I said.

"Here she is," Francis said.

I could hear voices in the background. Dee still hadn't come out of the shop so I waited by his car.

"Hello?" a small voice said.

"This is Marlon," I said.

"Do you have a wife named Suga?" the woman asked.

"Who wants to know?"

"I do. Nevermind who I am. I'm asking because your wife wanted me to call you. I wasn't sure if I had the right person or not… I'm still not sure."

"Yes, my wife is Suga. What do you know about my wife? Where is she?"

"I know that your wife is in danger."

"I know that much! Where is she?"

There was a pause.

"Answer me! Where is my wife?" I asked. I gripped the phone tighter.

"Calm down, I'm trying to help you! Do you know De'Angelo?"

When I heard her say Dee's real name I knew what information she was going to spill was going to be solid. No one called him by that name.

"Yeah, I know Dee. He got my wife?"

"Yeah, that's what she called him. I just know him by De'Angelo. I don't know much about what's going on. He told me that Suga broke into his house and he was teaching her a lesson. He made me think she was a junkie or something. I don't know where he is but I had to get out of there. I don't want to have anything to do with this. I told her I would call you and I did."

"Where is he holding her?"

"She was at his house the last time I saw her. I don't think she's going to be there long. He told me that he was going out of town for a while and we wouldn't be seeing each other for a while. I guess it was fun while it lasted."

"Is there a way you can get to my wife? Dee is with me. I can stall him if you can just get her out safely."

"I'm sorry I can't. I'm getting the hell out of here. I don't know if he's going to come for me now. I did my part. I told you where you can find your wife. I have to go."

"Wait!"

She hung up on me. I dialed the store back and Francis answered.

"Cole's Jewelry, how can I help you?" Francis said.

"Put her back on the phone!" I said.

"She's not here. She ran out of the store. What's going on?"

"Nothing. Everything is fine. Call me if you see her around."

"I sure will. If there is anything, and I mean anything that you need. Please let me know."

"I appreciate that. Thank you."

"No problem."

"Get home safe, Francis."

"I will."

I hung up the phone in frustration. I needed to get to Dee's house. I knew that he wasn't going to willingly take me there as long as Suga was there. I had to come up with something fast. Tomorrow was the exchange. I had to make a move tonight. If Dee went this far, he was willing to go further. He was going to kill Suga even if he got the money. I wasn't going to let that happen.

"Yo, Marlon! Do you want one of these fish sandwiches?"

The corner store beside the tire shop had the best fried fish and chicken on that side of the James River. I needed to call Linwood so that we could take Dee down.

"Yeah, grab me one. Unlock the door," I said.

I heard the doors of the car unlock. I watched Dee enter the corner store and then I got into the car. I called Linwood first.

"Hey, you were right. I just got confirmation. I know where she is," I said.

"Where is she?" Linwood asked.

"He was dumb enough to take her to his house. She's still alive."

"Are you still with him?"

"Yes, we have to make a move now. We can't let the sun come up on this."

"Were you supposed to pay tomorrow?"

"Yes, I'm going to call Ali too. We could use all the help we can get. I don't know who else is working with him."

"You're right. Give me the address. You keep him with you for as long as you can. I'm going to get my daughter."

"You've got to hurry and get her out of the house. I don't know how much longer I can keep him out here. Call me as soon as you get her out of there. Meet me back there as soon as you get her somewhere safe."

"I got this. Be safe."

I decided to stall Dee by having him drive me around town. There were still a few places that I could tell him that I wanted to check out. He was sure to believe that I didn't want to sit around and wait. The only problem was, he knew Suga was at his house and would want to get back to her as soon as he could. He already seemed like he was in a hurry. All I needed was for Linwood to get to Suga before Dee tried to get rid of me.

As I waited for Dee to come out of the store, two people ran by the car. I looked around to see what they were running from. Standing in front of the corner store was Gooch. He looked as if he would fall over if you blew on him. He was probably drunk or high. It was clear why the men were running. Gooch was probably stalking his next victim. No one wanted to be around him, including me. I respected him, but I didn't trust him. With all the hate, you never knew who paid the Grim Reaper to visit you.

I watched as Dee walked out the corner store, talking to a tall woman that looked like a runway model. He had his phone out and head down. He didn't look up before he bumped right into Gooch almost knocking him to the ground.

"Shit!" I said.

I didn't know what Gooch was up to. I didn't need them getting into anything that could cause Dee to lose his life before Suga was safe. Dee didn't even have his gun on him. I had to do something and fast. I got out of the car. Dee and Gooch were having words when I approached.

"Hey, what's up Gooch? Y'all good?"

"Hell no!" Gooch said.

"I apologized. I didn't see you," Dee said.

"You knocked my last cig out my hand. What are you going to do about it?" Gooch asked. I saw that hand of his move slowly towards his side.

"Wait. I have a fresh pack right here. You can have these," I said.

I handed Gooch the fresh pack of cigarettes. He reluctantly took them from me without taking his eyes off of Dee.

"Are we good?" I asked.

"We always good. But I'll be seeing you. I owe you," Gooch said.

"What the fuck you talking about? You owe me. We squared," Dee said.

I watched nervously as Gooch lit a cigarette. After a few tense moments, he walked away. Dee and I knew not to turn our backs on him; he had to leave first. I breathed a sigh of relief.

"Are you trying to get us killed?" I asked Dee.

"Man, that old man don't scare me. Fuck him," Dee said.

"Come on let's get from around here. I don't trust him," I said.

Dee and I headed back to his car. We both surveyed our surroundings, knowing how Gooch operated. As soon as we got in the car I had him open the compartment so that I could get my gun. I kept my gun in my hand. I didn't trust him and I knew that I wasn't safe around him. I was going to be ready when he decided to make a move.

"I'm not ready to go home yet. Let's check out a few more spots before I go home and wait this thing out," I said.

"I have to get back home. My sister is bringing Destiny home in a few," he said.

"It won't take too long. You don't have a problem with that, do you?"

"No, I'm good. I got you. I know you're probably nervous about tomorrow."

I felt Dee look over at me. I kept looking straight ahead. I didn't want to make him suspicious.

"You have no idea what I'm going through."

"Were you able to come up with the money for tomorrow?" he asked.

"I'm going to the bank first thing in the morning," I said.

"Good, I think you should give them what they want. Did you call the police yet?" he asked.

"Hell, no. I'm going to handle this myself. I'm going to pay them and get my baby back."

"That's what I'm talking about. I would've done the same thing."

"Do you think it was Trey's people?"

"I don't think so but those boys are wild. Come tomorrow we're going to find out. You don't have to worry about it because I'm going to handle that for you. You know you're my brother. I got you."

I didn't respond to him. I could no longer play this game with him. I kept thinking about Linwood and how he was going to get inside of Dee's house. I prayed that everything would go as planned. Tonight was the night of reckoning. Only one of us was going to see the sunrise and the other was going to meet their maker.

CHAPTER 18

Linwood

I stood over Trey's grave. It wasn't hard to find with the flat grave marker surrounded by alcohol bottles, flowers and snuffed out blunts surrounding the grave. It was evident that his homeboys paid him a few visits. I never understood why people left teddy bears, flowers and things like that at grave sites. Their loved ones were gone; they couldn't smell the flowers or appreciate sentimental items left behind. To each its own I guess.

"You dirty bitch! You tried to come for me! You came for my family. You sat in my face and plotted against me days before you ran up in my shit. I knew you weren't built for this life, but I took you under my wings. You took my trust and used it against me. You were going to take everything I worked for and have me come home to nothing. Now look at you, rotting away in the ground. I would say that's the perfect ending for a disloyal person like you. Burn in hell, bitch!"

I pulled out my dick and pissed all over his grave. I was sure to piss on his face on the grave marker.

"I told you, I'll piss on your grave," I said.

I didn't have much time to spare. I had to get to the address that Marlon gave me. I was familiar with the area and wasn't far. The only problem was that Mona was in the car waiting on me. I didn't have time to drop her off, so I had to let her know what was going on. This was going to let me know if she was ride or die for me or not.

"Hey, baby. Now do you feel better?" Mona asked. She placed a hand on my shoulder.

"No, but I did get some satisfaction from pissing on his grave," I said.

"No, you didn't! I know you didn't do something like that," she said.

We both looked at each other and laughed.

"Well, I guess he deserved it," she said.

"I have something to tell you."

"What's the matter, baby?"

"It's my daughter. I have to get to this address and get her out this house. Someone took her and is demanding money for her return?"

I handed her the paper that I wrote the address on. She looked at it and back at me.

"Oh my, God! Who would do something like that?"

"The one's closest to you. I don't have any time to waste. Let's go!"

Mona put the car in drive and sped off.

"Do you have a gun? How are you going to get her?" she asked.

"I stay strapped. Never leave home without. You just get me there," I said.

In less than fifteen minutes, we were driving slowly down the street where Dee lived. We parked three houses down from his. Mona turned off the car and we set there, staring at the house.

There was a vehicle in the driveway, but I knew that Dee was with Marlon. I came up with a way to get into the home based on my quick observation. My days of breaking and entering prepared me for this day.

"God, please let me save my baby girl," I said.

I stepped out of the car and walked towards the house with my gun in hand. I didn't care who saw me. If they decided to call the police and say that there was a crazy man with a gun, then the more the merrier. I didn't fear going back to prison. I would risk my life for my daughter.

As I approached, I looked for any signs of a home alarm system. There wasn't one. I walked to the front door and rang the doorbell. I waited and rang the bell again. I placed my ear to the door and listened. I didn't hear anything. The lights were on inside of the home. I looked inside of a window but couldn't see much. I didn't know who or how many accomplices he had. After no one came to the door, I walked around to the back of the house. I had to find a way in that wasn't so close to the street. I decided to go straight through the patio door. I picked up a stone garden turtle from the backyard and threw it at the patio glass door. I used the handle of a rake that was propped against the door to break out the rest of the glass. I entered the house.

"Hello? Is anybody here?" I asked. I moved slowly through the house letting my gun lead the way.

SNOOK

The house was quiet except the sound of music coming from upstairs. I made my way towards the stairs. I took each stair as quietly as possible. I was sure someone was up there. The music was loud and coming from behind closed doors. I took a deep breath and slowly approached. I put my ear to the door and all I could hear was the music.

I opened the door slowly. The room was pitch black. The light from the hall behind me allowed me to see a little. I used my hand to run along the wall to find a light switch. I felt one almost immediately. I switched the light on and prepared to blaze anything moving.

When the lights came on and my eyes adjusted, I saw Suga. She was handcuffed to the bed. She wasn't moving. I rushed over to her.

"Suga! Suga! Come on, baby!" I said.

I shook her violently by her shoulders. No response. Her head was bandaged and she was bleeding through her bandage.

"No! Wake up. Daddy is here. Come on, Suga! Breathe for me!"

I began to give her mouth to mouth. I didn't care if I was doing it wrong as long as I tried. I wasn't able to move her much with her hand being handcuffed. I looked around for something to free her. There wasn't anything that could help. I held the gun close to the chain of the handcuff and fired.

Suga took a breath and woke up screaming.

"No! Help! Help!" she screamed. Her voice was strained.

"It's me, Suga. I got you, baby. Daddy is here," I said.

"Daddy? Linwood? Is that you? Where did you come from?" she asked.

"It's me. I'm home. I came to get you out of here," I said.

She grabbed me and held me tightly. My heart melted as I held her tighter.

"Thank you!" she sobbed.

"We have to get out of here, now."

"Where is Dee? He's going to kill us!"

She became frantic and began to panic.

"No, he's not. Marlon has him."

I helped her to her feet. She had a hard time holding herself up. I had to pick her up in my arms and carry her out of the house. She held on tightly. For once in a very long time, I felt needed. She needed me and I was there for her.

Mona pulled up as soon as we reached the street. Suga and I sat in the back while Mona drove. Suga was quiet as she lay in my arms. I held her close to me.

"Is she okay? Do we need to go to the hospital?" Mona asked.

"Yes," I said.

I felt Suga shift uncomfortably in my arms but she didn't object.

When we pulled up to the hospital, I got out and ran inside. I returned with a nurse and wheelchair. Mona was helping Suga out of the car. Right then, I knew she was ride or die for me. The nurse rushed over to assist Mona. Mona met my eyes.

"Can you stay with her?" I asked.

"Of course, go handle your business. I have her," she said.

"Are you sure you got this?" I asked.

She gave me a knowing look and I understood.

"I'll let them know how I found her passed out in her home," Mona said.

I gave her a quick kiss and whispered in her ear, "Stick to that story no matter what."

I headed to Marlon. This wasn't over. To see the pain and condition that Suga was in had me in tears. This was her second brush with death. I knew she was going to be messed up behind this. As if she didn't already have enough to deal with. This had to end once and for all. I called Marlon.

"It's done. She's safe," I said.

"Okay, sounds good. See you soon," he said.

"I'm on the way."

"That'll work."

I knew he was talking in code, because he was around Dee. I just prayed that Marlon kept his head on straight. Whatever he had planned for Dee, he had to do it quickly. This situation couldn't be dragged out any longer. Marlon wanted to kill Dee, but I had to get in on the action too.

CHAPTER 19

Dee

We drove around the city for over an hour. I was getting bored looking at Marlon's sad face while he tried to search for Suga. I knew it was all in vain because only I knew where she was. I couldn't wait to get rid of him and get back to the house. I still had to prepare for tomorrow. Suga was going to take her last breath tonight. I was going to collect my money and start a new life with my daughter. I was done with Richmond. There was nothing else here for me. I was growing agitated with taking Marlon's orders.

"I have to get home. Did you want me to drop you off at home?" I asked.

"I'm not ready to go home yet. I'll go to your house," Marlon said.

I swallowed hard. There was no way I was taking him back to my house.

"Once I get Destiny, I'm in the house for the night. I might as well drop you off now."

"I'm not ready to go home. I haven't seen Destiny in a while. Let's just go to your house. What's the problem?"

Marlon looked at me strangely.

"It's not a problem. It's just that the house isn't straight and I didn't plan on coming back out tonight," I said.

"Don't worry. I'll catch an Uber," he said.

He sat back in his seat and seemed to relax. I ran out of excuses and tried to come up with a quick plan. Instead of fighting him on this, I complied. As we drove to my house, I formulated a plan to keep Marlon outside long enough to move Suga to the basement. I sent Lex on her way and prayed that she wouldn't say anything about what happened at my house. In the back of mind, something told me to kill her too, but I had only prepared for the disposal of one body, not two. I had called Lex several times and she didn't answer which made me really think she would turn on me. But after she sent me a text that she loved me, I relaxed enough to clear my conscience.

Marlon was acting differently. I knew that he was going through some emotional turmoil because of Suga's situation and all, but it wasn't that. For a moment, I thought that maybe he was on to me. I took every precaution to make sure that I didn't show my hand and to get the spotlight off of me. I know I didn't fuck that up. I threw the car into park as soon as we arrived at my house.

"Give me about five minutes to clean up a little before you come in. The house has been a mess since Kendra left me," I said.

"She didn't leave you. She died," he said.

"You know what I mean. It's been rough being Mr. Mom, you know."

"I don't want to know. That is why I'm going to get Suga back so that I don't have to raise my child alone."

I took in a deep breath.

"Just give me five minutes," I said.

I quickly walked to the door and rushed inside. The house was still quiet. I ran upstairs and saw that the light was on in the room where I left Suga. My heart fell in my ass. I slowly pushed the door open to find that she was gone. The bed was empty.

"Fuck!"

I panicked. She was gone and I didn't know where. There wasn't any police outside so she had to still be in the house.

"You bitch! Where are you?" I shouted.

I ran out of the room and checked all of the rooms upstairs. I checked under beds and in closets. She wasn't there. I didn't have much time to look for her and hide her. Things were falling apart.

I rushed downstairs to look for her. I walked into the kitchen. That was when I noticed that the patio door was broken. I ran out to the patio and looked around the backyard. She was gone.

What the fuck am I going to do now?

I walked back into the house as I tried to think of what to do next.

"You know what's funny, Dee?" Marlon asked in a flat, cold tone startling me.

SNOOK

He stood in my living room with his gun pointed at me. I put my hands up.

"What the fuck are you doing?" I asked.

"Toss your gun. Slowly," he said.

I did what he asked. I slowly removed my gun and slid it across the floor away from the both of us.

"You know what's up. Suga was found in your house. What do you know about that?" he asked, walking closer to me.

"What are you talking about? I didn't have anything to do with Suga going missing! You know me. I would never betray you like that," I pleaded. "I didn't have anything to do with what happened to Suga. I'm being set up. I'm the one that has been down for you!"

"Who else did you get involved in this? Who's helping you?" Marlon asked.

"Nobody is helping me do nothing because I ain't did shit. Come on fool. If I was going to get you for your paper, I'll come for you, not Suga. That's too much work," I said.

"Naw, that's just what you would do. I know you have a thing for my wife. You always have. She wouldn't touch you with the next bitch's dirty pussy," Marlon said.

I laughed at his arrogance. He thought that he had his sweet innocent wife all to himself. It was time to let him know what kind of wife Suga really was.

"What the fuck is so funny?" he asked.

"She wouldn't touch me with the next bitch's dirty pussy," I said mocking him. "Why would she when she let me get all up in her sweet pussy. I know you said she was good but that was an understatement. Suga got her name honestly. Yeah, I fucked your wife every chance I could once she found out about you and Kendra. I stuck my dick in every hole in her body and she loved it! That's what you did with Kendra, right?" I said.

"You dirty dick bitch! You wish you could have my wife. She would never sleep with someone like you," Marlon shouted.

"No, I had her. I even had her in your house," I said.

He drew back and cracked me across my head with his gun, sending me to the floor.

"Ugh!" I shrieked.

I felt the metal open my flesh and then pain instantly shot through my head.

"Yeah, you think I didn't see you fuck Kendra that night at your apartment. I was there. I saw the two of you. The only thing that kept her alive was the fact that she was pregnant and she kept you alive so that we could stay in your pockets with blackmail. I knew all about it," I said.

"Your slut for a wife always wanted this dick. I guess you knew that too. If you were there, you would know that I was drunk. She took advantage of me," he said.

I was over it. I was going to die. I accepted that. I knew that I wasn't going to get out of the house alive. I wanted to fire shots at Marlon with my words. I had one more round for his ass.

"If you did fuck her, I hope it was worth it. Your ass is going to die tonight. You were…" he said.

I cut him off and said, "It was worth it. Worth seeing you squirm at the hospital when you thought that maybe your son wasn't yours. I saw you. It was a possibility that he could've been mine. That's why I wanted to make sure that Suga knew that I was going to be there for my son if he was mine. Oh, but you picked up on that too. I heard you had that DNA test done. Congratulations," I said.

Marlon let out a crazy laugh. He laughed so hard he was holding his stomach. I thought he was going to go crazy and shoot everything up.

"I get it now. Your psychotic ass wanted my life and your slimy ass killed L.C., didn't you?" he asked.

It was my turn to laugh. Now I laughed in his face.

"You finally figured it out. It took you long enough. The police are even dumber than you. You should've been locked up by now for those murders. Instead, they came after Suga," I said.

"So, you took the money for yourself and set me up for murder," Marlon said.

"Yeah, that's what I did. Fuck you!" I shouted.

"After I moved your ungrateful ass out that dirty ass trap house your momma had you living in, this is how you repay me? You were fucking Kendra's ass on your pissy ass mattress until I showed you how to get money. When I ate, you ate! You were supposed to be my brother. I always made sure you and your family had. I offered you the opportunity to go in on the store and you didn't. You'd rather stay in the streets than make honest money. Yet, I still gave to you because you were my brother; my family," Marlon said.

"You didn't give enough. I ate your crumbs long enough. You looked down on me like me and my family wasn't shit.

You and your bitch thought you were better than us. I stopped feeling like family a long time ago. You don't mean no more to me than anyone else out here," I said.

Marlon looked at me as if I was shit on the bottom of his shoe. That was exactly how I felt being in his shadow. Finally, I let him know how I really felt. He didn't mean shit to me. I was drained. I'd said everything that I needed to say. I played all of my cards all in one hand. I had nothing else to give.

I knew Marlon didn't have the heart to take me out. But after admitting to being with Suga, he might've grown the balls to do it. I had to get the best of him. At this point, I had to take Marlon out and forget about the money. My plans just went south.

Santé

When we arrived at the hospital, it was chaotic. There were several ambulance and police cars at the emergency entrance. Ali fought his way through the traffic to get me as close as possible to the entrance. I watched the people come and go in and out of the hospital. I never liked hospitals. It always represented death. Some people go and never come out.

After a few grueling minutes of stop and go traffic, we were close enough for me to walk the rest of the way. Ali let me out close to the emergency room entrance and went to find a parking space. I didn't care if or how long it took him to find one, I had to get to Suga. I felt so bad for her. She'd been through so much in such a short period of time. I had a few minutes to be alone with her before Ali joined us.

I rushed inside of the hospital to find a long line of people waiting for patient information. I waited impatiently as the line dwindled down one by one. It moved quicker than I had anticipated. Finally, I was next.

Before the woman behind the desk could properly greet me I said, "Hello. I'm here to see Suga Cole. She was brought here about an hour ago."

"Let me see," the woman said. She typed something into her computer. "Please spell the person's first name for me."

I proceeded to spell Suga's name.

"Yes, she's here. She's being moved to a room right now."

She wrote something down on a small piece of paper. "Here's the room number." She slid the paper across the desk.

"Thank you," I said. I grabbed the paper and rushed towards the elevator.

I didn't know how I was going to explain to her that Ali was going to rob the store in the morning. If it wasn't for me, it wouldn't be happening because it was my idea. I needed her to know that I was sorry and that I was going to stop him if I could. I really needed to tell her about my drug addiction. That was how he controlled me.

I reached the third floor and looked for her room number. I rushed into the room and found Suga being helped into her bed by a nurse. There was another woman standing by as if she was guarding her. She looked at me as if I didn't belong there. I stopped halfway into the room. The woman walked quickly towards me.

"Can I help you?" the woman asked.

"No, I don't think so. She's my cousin," I said.

"I'm a friend of her father's and he wanted me to look out for her until he gets back."

I knew who she was. My uncle had told me all about this

woman that he'd fallen in love with before he came home. I didn't know much about her, but she seemed to have his back.

"Her father is my uncle. I'm Santé," I said.

"I know who you are. He talks about you just as much as he talks about his daughter. Thanks for picking him up for me. I wasn't able to take off early to get him."

"No problem at all."

I looked around her to see what Suga was doing. The nurse was placing a blood pressure cuff on her arm.

"How is she?" I asked.

"She's severely dehydrated, she has a concussion, her arm is fractured and she has some infected wounds."

"Wounds? What did he do to her?"

"I'm not sure, but she has plenty of bruises on her body. She hasn't said much. The doctors are asking a lot of questions."

"What did she tell them?"

"We said that we found her passed out at her home. That accounts for the gash and concussion that she has, but not all of the other bruises she has. I think that they are getting suspicious."

"We are going to have to get her out of here soon. I'm sure Marlon can get her a nurse. Let's wait until we hear from one of them before we make any decisions."

"Good idea. Knowing Linwood, it's best that we stay here for now. We don't know what's going on."

"You got that right."

"Santé? Is that you?" Suga called out.

Mona and I rushed to Suga's side.

I grabbed her hand and said, "Yes, it's me. I'm right here."

She smiled with her eyes closed.

The nurse continued to attach her to the numerous machines around her bed.

"Is she in pain?" I asked the nurse.

"Yes, she's in pain. We're giving her fluids and pain medication," she assured me.

"Hey, girl," Suga said. Her voice was weak and almost inaudible.

"Hey," I replied.

She gripped my hand tightly.

"Where's Marlon? Where's my son?" she asked.

"Don't worry, they both are safe. I promise you everything is going to be okay," I said.

I squeezed her hand to let her know that I meant it. She squeezed my hand back. I knew that she understood.

"If there is anything you need, please let me know," the nurse said. She handed Suga the remote with the nurse call button. She didn't reach for it so I placed it beside her.

"Thank you," Suga said.

"No problem. I will be next door if she needs me," the nurse said.

"I hope to never see you again. This is too soon to be back in here," Suga said.

"I hope to never see you under these circumstances again. You are such a beautiful person. I hope that you get all the healing you need while you are here. I will be back to check on you," the nurse said.

With that, I saw tears fall from Suga's eyes. I grabbed a tissue from the table and wiped her tears. She opened her eyes as much as she could.

"I was just here fighting for my life. I was almost gone. If I had died, my son would have been a motherless child, just like me. Now look at me. My sins landed me back in this hospital bed. It's sad that it took for all of this to happen for me to realize what's important. My family is all I need. I don't care about nothing else. All of the money, the house, diamonds and clothes didn't mean anything. I love my husband. I want to be with him and no one else. I know that he loves me too. I've decided that I'm going to let him love me. That is something that I never let happen. I'm going to love him and let him love me. No more secrets and no more lies," Suga said.

"You know that Marlon loves you. You're a great mother and wife. All you need to do is get better and take care of your family. That's all," I assured her.

"No. I need help. There are some things that I can't do on my own. With God, I will overcome those things."

"I know you will. You have everyone's support."

I consoled her the best that I could as she wept. I wasn't sure what all transpired in her life that caused her to weep so deeply. Other than being kidnapped and having Lord knows what done to her during that time, she had been through it and she was releasing it all. The bad part was that there was more bad news coming. I had to find a way to warn her, but I didn't know if it was the right time. Her condition was worse than I thought.

"Ladies, I'm going to step out. Do you want anything?" Mona asked.

She looked as if she had been crying. I know I shed a few tears.

"No, thank you," I said.

"Ginger Ale, please," Suga said. "My throat is so dry."

"Okay. I'll see if I can grab you something to put on your stomach too," Mona said.

"Thank you," Suga said.

We were now alone. Ali was due to walk in at any moment. I knew that if I didn't talk to her now, we won't have another time we would be alone. I was scared and nervous. I didn't know how she was going to respond. I fought back my own tears as I prepared myself to tell Suga the plan. I watched as her eyes fluttered. It appeared that whatever medication they gave her was starting to take effect.

"Suga, can you hear me?" I asked.

"Yes, what's the matter?" she asked.

She probably heard the nervousness in my voice. I realized that I was now squeezing her hand with both of mine.

"I have something to tell you," I said.

"You know that you can tell me anything. Nothing has changed between us. We're still like sisters," she said.

My stomach sunk with her words. I knew that we always had that bond. I was the one that betrayed her and I had to wear that. After this, there was no turning back.

"You know what Ali does, right?" I asked.

"Of course. You already told me that," she said.

"Well, I told him about your store."

"What about my store?"

I felt her pull her hand away. She tried to open her eyes to look at me. She peered at me with her eyes half opened.

"I know you didn't turn him on to my store... Is he trying to rob us?" she asked.

She tried to sit up. She groaned in agony. I jumped up to try to keep her from hurting herself more.

"No, don't sit up. You're going to hurt yourself. Lay back down, please," I said.

She fought against me, but lost the fight. She didn't have the strength. She gave in and laid back down.

"I can't believe you! How could you do that to me?" she said.

"I'm sorry. I didn't mean to. One night, he got me high and it kind of came out that way. After he had it stuck in his mind he wouldn't let it go. I tried to talk him out of it several times but he isn't listening to me."

"So now he's getting you high and you done lost your damn mind. How long have this been going on?"

I lowered my head in shame.

"For a while now. But I'm not an addict. I can say no," I said.

"Really? I guess this Ali character isn't all that he seemed to be. I can't believe you!" she said.

"I'm sorry! That's why I had to tell you. I never meant to hurt you. I knew that you had insurance."

"Are you serious? Insurance cost money! It's going to cost even more money if we are robbed, stupid. This could ruin us! I guess you thought this all the way through."

The look she gave me made my skin crawl. She was disgusted with me and hurt.

"I'm so sorry. I wasn't thinking clearly," I said.

"You're right about that! You let him get you hooked on drugs. I didn't know you were so weak. What happened to your dreams of going to New York and modeling? You get to

New York and hook up with the first no good man that shows you some attention. Now look at you!"

I was now becoming enraged. She was coming for me and hitting below the belt right now was not called for. She wasn't better than me. She was only where she was because of Marlon's hard work. If you remove him from the equation, she'd be nowhere.

"I know that you think that you're better than me, but you're not. If it wasn't for your husband you wouldn't be anywhere near where you are now. I know you think you're better than me, but you're not. You're out here trying to find your way. Everything you have is because of Marlon. You're no more than a gold digger!"

"Get out! Get out right now! Don't think I'm not going to notify the police about you and your criminal boyfriend conspiring to rob my business. You best run back to New York where you belong. As long as you are in Virginia, you will never be safe," she said.

"Are you threatening me?" I asked.

"Did you conspire against me? What did you think? I was going to take it lying down. If you were any family of mine you would've never plotted against me. Get lost Santé."

I stood to my feet. I heard someone enter the room. I was relieved that it was only Mona. I didn't know how much she heard of our conversation.

"Is everything okay in here?" Mona asked.

She had what looked like a bag of cafeteria food and bottle drinks.

"Yeah, we're good. I'm about to leave. Be sure to look after her," I said.

I walked slowly towards the door. Before I reached the door Suga said, "Be sure to leave my money."

"Mona, please close the door. I don't want these strangers coming in and out of my room. You can't trust anyone these days," Suga said.

"Sure, honey. You need to rest," Mona said.

I looked back at her and didn't say a word. I had planned to leave the money with her anyway. After the way she talked to me, I was thinking about changing my mind. I was so angry with her that I didn't care what happened. I couldn't have her calling the police, not with all that was going on.

CHAPTER 21

Marlon

He had to die. He stole from me, lied, fucked my wife and set me up for murder. I couldn't believe the very person that I loved and trusted the most, was my enemy. I was hurt by everything that he had said and done. I wasn't going to let him know it by losing my cool. I had to keep my head and do what I had to do.

"Get up!" I said.

Dee slowly stood to his feet attempting to raise both hands in the air. He struggled to raise his arm with his injured shoulder. I looked him in his eyes and all I saw was evil. I never knew how much hate he had in his heart for me but now it was clear. I raised my gun and pointed at his head.

"After everything we've been through, this is how it ends," Dee said.

"You did this," I said.

"No! You did this! You was on that Nino Brown shit, but

you couldn't see it. Even when I die, you have to live with the fact that you treated me no better than a stray. You met Suga and everything changed. You changed. What happened to our plans? What happened to everything we said we were going to do when we grew up? You forgot all about me."

"We aren't kids anymore. We did some shit together, but we had to grow up."

"If that's what you call it. I call it growing apart. I guess this is where it ends, me at your mercy. I guess I'm supposed to beg for my life now. That's what you expect me to do, right?"

"I don't expect you to do anything. Just lay down and die."

"Fuck you then! Kill me. Go ahead. I want to see you do it. You ain't never had the heart to pull the trigger. I did that for you! You ain't shit without me!"

"Fuck you. Die bitch!"

I aimed and fired. My ears begin to ring. Dee grabbed the side of his face in agony. Blood shot from his face where I shot him.

"You shot me!" he yelled.

"I needed you to know that I had the heart to pull the trigger," I said.

"Marlon, I'm sorry. Please don't kill me, man. I'll do anything, please don't kill me!"

Dee was begging for his life. I wasn't moved. He tried to get away from me. I was on his heels still aiming for his head. Seeing him scramble away was pure entertainment. I wanted to see him suffer. The front door to Dee's home was forced opened, sending the door slamming against the wall. The both of us was startled as we looked towards the door. I kept an eye on Dee as I backed against the wall. I watched to see who was at the door. I assumed it was the police.

"Who the fuck is it?" I shouted.

There wasn't an answer. I didn't hear anything. I moved around to get a view of the front door, but could still keep an eye on Dee. I slowly moved my gun from Dee towards the door when I heard footsteps.

"It's me, man," a familiar voice said.

My adrenaline was rushing and my mind raced as I tried to place the voice. Before I could figure out whose voice I heard, I saw Gooch around the corner. He was swaying like a drunk. He took several missteps, almost falling over.

"What the fuck are you doing in my house?" Dee asked.

I moved the gun from Dee to Gooch. Gooch laughed and stood straight up with a straight face. He no longer appeared drunk and out of it. He stood tall and strong. That was when I noticed the gun in his hand.

"I'm here to finish a job," Gooch said.

He looked over at Dee who was still holding his bleeding face.

"What? Gooch, what are you doing here?" I asked.

Gooch didn't acknowledge my question.

"It's time for me to fulfill my contract. I killed your bitch now it's your turn," Gooch said to Dee.

"That was you? You shot me! You killed my wife!" Dee said.

"I never miss my target. It wasn't your time to go. You had to suffer first. But, now your time is up," Gooch said.

"You killed my wife!" Dee said.

He charged towards Gooch. He didn't take more than two steps before Gooch blew his brains all over the wall.

SNOOK

Dee's body collapsed near my feet. I looked down as blood leaked out of his head towards me. I stepped back from the blood. When I looked up, Gooch was walking away. I didn't know what to say. Dee was dead, but not by my hands. I wanted to be the one to end his life, but that was taken from me. I was relieved that Gooch didn't come for me.

Now I had a dead body on my hands. I was sure that the neighbors called the police. It was a matter of minutes before they arrived. The nightmare was almost over.

"Marlon!" Linwood called out.

"In here!" I said.

He came rushing inside of the house.

"I thought Gooch killed your ass!" Linwood said.

He looked down at Dee's lifeless body. He let out a short laugh.

"Damn! Did he do this? Gooch out here still putting in work," he said.

"Where have you been? You were supposed to meet me here. You were supposed to have my back," I said.

"When I got here I saw this old car sitting on the street. I didn't see anybody sitting in the car. That's when Gooch held me at gun point. He put me in the trunk. He just let me go. What in the hell does Gooch have to do with all of this?" he asked.

"This shit is crazy. Gooch killed Kendra and let Dee live. He came here to finish the job. We saw him earlier right before coming here. He must've followed us here."

Standing over Dee's body, we both looked down at him. Linwood signaled for me to step out of the room to talk. I followed behind him.

"So, what is the plan now?" I asked.

"Burn this bitch down," he said.

"Yeah, let's do it."

"I'm not going to let you go out like this. I can't. My daughter and my grandson needs you. Let me take care of this. This is easy, son. Let me do this for you."

The nightmare was finally over. I wanted to hold my son and see my wife. I had to see about Suga. I knew she was at the hospital being cared for, but I knew she needed me. Linwood tossed me his keys.

"You need to get out of here. My car is parked down the street. Leave out the back," he said."

"Do you need help?" I asked.

"No, I got it."

"Thank you."

"No need for that, you're family. We do what we have to do to protect our family."

"Yes, we do. I have to check on Suga. Are you sure you're okay with this?"

"Go to my daughter. Get out of here."

"Are you sure?"

"Yes. Go!"

Although, I felt that leaving Linwood to clean up the mess was selfish, I had to go. I trusted that he could take care of things. My trust level for anyone was non-existent. Although I trusted someone that I shouldn't have trusted, I decided to trust Linwood to get the job done.

CHAPTER 22

Suga

I woke up in a cold sweat from a nightmare that left me fighting for my life. Dee was standing over me with Junior in his arms, threatening to drop him off of a rooftop. I begged and pleaded with him while he laughed and Junior cried. I woke up right when he let him go.

"Are you okay?" I heard my Uncle Redd ask.

I looked at him and tried to sit up to hug him.

"Now just relax. You can't be moving around like that," he said.

He gave me a hug and I held him tightly. I smelled him and took in his scent.

"Save some of that love for me," Marlon said.

"Baby!" I said.

I let go of my uncle.

"I know you want to see your husband, let me get my kiss and move out of the way," Redd said.

He gave me a quick kiss on the cheek and moved to the other side of the room. Marlon was standing there so handsome. I could see the stress on his face. I smiled when I saw him and my heart melted when he smiled back. There was no doubt that he loved me, even with all of my flaws. I felt his love and I returned it. We embraced each other tightly.

Marlon sat down beside me and moved my hair from my face. He kissed me deeply. I wrapped my arms around his neck tightly and held him. I never wanted to be away from him again. He held onto me as we both savored the moment. His touch soothed my aching heart and sealed my feelings towards him. Everything I felt for him, I felt it in return. To let down my guard and allow him to love me and accept it was the best feeling in the world. Love was a powerful feeling. It felt better than money, designer clothes, shoes, bags and diamonds; those were the things that I once loved more than anything.

"We can't keep meeting like this little lady," Marlon said.

"If it were up to me we wouldn't be here at all. Where have you been? Is everything all right?" I asked in a whisper.

"No more worries. We're good," he said.

"Where's our son? I miss him so much. Where is he?" I asked.

"He's safe with my mother. He's on the way. You're going to be here another day or so. But if you want to leave, I can talk to the doctors and arrange for you to be cared for at home."

"Yes, I'm ready to go home."

Uncle Redd jumped up and volunteered to talk to the doctor.

"I'll go and talk to the doctor about moving you home to be cared for. I'm sure that you all have some catching up to do. And the next time my baby is in trouble, you need to let me know what's going on. Don't you ever leave me in the dark like that again," Uncle Redd said to Marlon.

"Yes, sir. I apologize for that," Marlon said.

Uncle Redd gave Marlon a stern look and then smiled and winked at me. I guess he knew what happened to me. I didn't know how much he knew about what was going on. I didn't know how much Marlon knew about me and Dee. I wanted my past far behind me. I wasn't the same person I was before this. I didn't know what was going on while I was held captive. I didn't know if Marlon called the police and they were out there looking for me or who in my family was aware that I was missing. All I knew was that Marlon was going to do whatever it took to find me. That was something that I was sure about.

"I'll be right back," Uncle Redd said.

As soon as he left the room I said, "We have to talk."

"Now what?" he sighed.

"Santé and Ali is planning to rob the store. She had the nerve to confess to me that she was the one that came up with the idea. If I wasn't hurting so bad, I would've beat her ass," I said.

"Wait a minute, Ali has been here helping me find you and Santé been running around acting like she cared about what happened to you, yet they're planning to rob our store?" Marlon said.

He jumped up from the bed and said, "I'm tired of this shit! People think that they can keep coming for mine!"

"Baby, please calm down! Come here," I said. I reached for him.

After pacing the floor a few more times, he came to me. I held his hands in mine. We looked into each other's eyes and I saw rage. I thought that I was the one suffering the worst from everything that had been going on, but I saw the toll that all of this was taking on him.

"I don't think she's stupid enough to let Ali go through with it now that she's told me about the robbery. Don't worry. At best, she's on her way back to New York with him and her drug habit," I said.

"He got her on drugs?" Marlon asked.

"He sure does. As soon as she came out her mouth with that shit, I knew she had to have been getting high. After this, she is out of my life. I just want my money and her out of my life for good," I said.

"What money?" he asked.

"Marlon, it's time for me to be honest about a few things. At my father's house, I found his money and some other things. I took it all. I had Santé sell the items I found and I hid the cash in our garage. At the time I wasn't sure where we were going in our marriage. I trusted you, but then I didn't trust you. I wanted to make sure that if things ended between us, I would be able to take care of Junior," I explained.

"I found the money in the garage. That's how I knew that you didn't leave me."

"I'm so sorry. There's so much you just don't know about me. I've done some really fucked up things..."

"I don't care what you've done. I love you, Suga. We're going to get through all of this. I've made mistakes too. You're not the only one to blame in all of this. Just promise me that we are moving forward, together. Let's leave the past in the past. After today, we have a new life together."

"But, you don't understand…"

He placed his pointer finger on my lips and said, "Hush. I understand that you have been through a traumatizing event and now you want to confess all of your sins. I don't care. Let that be between you and God. We are starting over, fresh."

"This has really changed me. Thinking that I would never see you again, touch you again. It was too much. I know what love is," I said.

"I love you, Suga."

"I love you more, Marlon."

"I love you more."

"No, I love you more."

We both laughed. I sat back on the bed and looked into his eyes. The stress that I once saw seemed to be lifting. Things between us felt right for the first time in a long time. I relished in the moment.

"I have to handle this thing with your cousin. Let me make a few phone calls. I promise I will be right back. I got this. I got us," he said.

I waited almost fifteen minutes for Marlon to return. I prayed that he didn't do anything stupid, like try to stop them himself. I was alone and feeling anxious. The door to my hospital room opened slowly. I looked towards the door. I thought it was Uncle Redd returning.

"Surprise!"

Uncle Redd, Alyssa, Mona and Linwood came into my room with balloons and cake.

"What is all of this?" I asked.

"It's your birthday. Did you forget?" Uncle Redd asked.

"I must've. With everything that's going on, I forgot all about my birthday. But thank you."

"Hey, baby girl," my father said.

"Hi, Dad," I said. The word "Dad" felt a little foreign on my tongue.

His smile brightened when I said that.

"When you get a chance, we need to talk," he said.

I already knew what he wanted to talk about. He wanted to know where his money went. The money was his. Since seeing him, I knew that I had to give it all back. I gave him a knowing look and he smiled. Seeing my father with Mona and Uncle Redd with Alyssa made me smile. They both looked so happy with their significant others.

Celebrating my birthday with my family was everything. I'd lost track of time while being held by Dee. When my mother-in-law arrived with my son, the tears came and wouldn't stop. My son was more handsome than I remembered. In those few days, he had changed. He was still the perfect blend of me and his father, but his little personality was so bright. I missed out on so much bonding time with him, that all I could do was weep and hold him close to me. He looked me in my eyes and smiled a few times. It surprised me how alert he was. He fit so perfectly in my arms. Our bond was still strong. It was an amazing feeling. I vowed to never let anything or anyone come between me and my family ever again.

CHAPTER 23

Santé

As Ali threw his belongings into a suitcase on the hotel bed, I watched from a distance. I'd confessed that I'd confided in Suga about our plans and he went ballistic. He struck me twice before he was able to get a hold of himself. I saw the disappointment on everyone else's faces when they found out that they came all the way down here for nothing. All of this just to go back home without their prize.

"I can't believe you screwed us like this. After all of the preparation we made for this, I trusted you and you betrayed me," Ali said.

"I told you that I didn't want to do this anymore and you wouldn't listen to me. How can I do that to her after all she'd been through? That would've been malicious of me," I said.

"So what were you when you came up with the plan to rob your cousin? This was your plan remember?" he said.

"I was high. You'd been getting me high and I wasn't thinking straight. As soon as it left my mouth, I wanted to take it back. It was too late. You were all over it. I wanted to impress you and show you that I could be part of the crew too. I see now that I'm not really built for this. This is your life, not mine."

"You're just seeing that? I never asked you to be part of the crew. I wanted you to be my girl. You never needed to fit in with the crew. As long as you were mine your status was above the crew. You didn't know that?"

I thought about what he said for a moment. I thought that if I was able to help him with his business he would love me even more. I saw how meticulous he was and how each score moved him up in his business. I wanted to help him. I wanted to solidify myself in his life as his woman and his business partner. I know now that it was all wrong.

"I'm sorry, my family is more important to me than anything," I said.

"After what you told me she said to you, do you think she gives a fuck about you right now?" he asked.

"Why wouldn't she be mad? Anyone would be mad about that. Yes, she said some hurtful things to me, but at the end of the day that's my family. She may never trust me again, but we have no choice but to move on from this. You don't think I'm mad as hell about what she said to me?"

"I'm sure you are, Santé. You're so mad that you're going to just hop your ass in the car and drive back to the top with what you left with."

"Yes, I'm going back to New York with everything I came

here with. Every last dollar of that money I made for her. I still have it and I'm taking it back with us."

Ali stopped packing and finally looked at me. I watched a smile creep across his face.

"You still have all the money? How much did you make? You never told me," he asked.

"I was able to get fifteen thousand dollars from the guy you hooked me up with. You said that he would do right by me off the strength of your relationship with him, and he did. He gave me top dollar. I took twenty percent for myself."

"Are you planning to give the money to her? Since you're all in your feelings and shit."

"Hell no. I'm taking it. We can break the crew off and keep the rest. I don't care about the money."

"That's still chump change compared to what we could've scored. Let's pack up and get out of here. They could've notified the police by now. We have to leave quickly and quietly."

Ali's mood changed quickly with the news of the money. For a moment, I thought he was going to leave my ass here to deal with this mess alone. I knew that the crew was upset with me, but they will get over it with a few stacks in their hands.

I jumped up and hugged him. We kissed and confirmed our love for each other. He looked toward the table where we'd done coke the night before. After I left the hospital, I was so distraught that all I wanted to do was get high. The coke numbed me and I didn't give two fucks about anyone or anything. That was the point.

"Wait a minute, I have something special for you," he said.

"What I had last night was fine. Isn't that the rest of it?" I asked, pointing to the white powder left in a baggie on the table.

"Yes, but I've been saving something special just for you. I was saving it for our celebration after we got the jewels, but we can celebrate now," he said.

A feeling of uneasiness crept over me. I wasn't sure what he was talking about. I didn't think much of it at first.

"What are you waiting for? Pack up," he said.

I'd already had my things packed from the night before. I pulled my suitcases out of the closet and placed them by the front door. I headed into the bathroom to pack up my makeup and hair products. When I came out, I noticed Ali adding something from a baggie to what coke was left out on the table. I'd assumed that he was adding more for himself. I proceeded to finish packing. When I was done, I walked over to the table to join Ali.

"Are you ready?" he asked.

"Sure is. This one is for the road," I said.

I watched him separate three neat lines of coke. I noticed that the coke wasn't completely white as it had been before. It was tinged with a beige color.

"What did you put in it?" I asked.

"It's my special blend. Go ahead, try it," he said.

"Are you going to have some?"

"Yeah, right after you."

I felt the hair on the back of my neck stand up. The look on his face told me that I shouldn't trust him. Instead of listening to my instincts, I snorted each one of the two lines of what I believed to be coke.

"Where's the money?" he asked.

It didn't take long for me to feel the high. This time, it felt different. The usual energetic feeling I get when snorting coke didn't come. I felt a high that I'd never felt before.

"What is this?" I asked. I could tell that my speech was becoming slurred, because it was difficult getting out those few words.

"Where is the money?" Ali asked.

He turned to walk away from me and I tried to reach for him. I watched him walk over to the door to where my bags were and began to search them.

"What are you doing?" I asked.

"You betrayed me. You did the one thing that I asked you never to do. You came between me and my money," he said.

I heard his words, but couldn't respond. I watched as he pulled out the bag that held the money. He looked back at me and smiled.

I began to feel warm and drowsy. I fought to keep my eyes open as I began to lose consciousness. I was fighting to stay awake. I slumped down in the chair as I struggled to gain control, but lost.

CHAPTER 24

Linwood

Seeing Suga in the hospital, brought things into perspective. My absence played a major role as to why Suga had so many problems in her life. The absence of her mother made it even worse. Redd did all that he could to raise her right, but the damage was already done. Only Teesa and I could attempt to undo the damage that we'd caused our child. I could still see the hurt and pain in her eyes. I could see the longing for my love and yearning for her mother. I was only one bad decision away from being taken from her again. Kyle was still on my shit list. As badly as I wanted to get at him, I decided that being present in Suga's life was more important than revenge.

I was a free man. If I wanted to remain a free man I had to let that one go. Kyle was someone else's problem. I was sure that I wasn't the only one that he'd done dirty in his career. There was sure to be more clients that he screwed. I decided to let it go. Suga was released from the hospital and back home recovering from her ordeal. Instead of bringing Mona along, I went to see her on my own.

"Hey, Pops," Marlon said greeting me with a manly hug.

It felt good to be greeted so warmly by him.

"Hey, son," I replied.

"Suga has been waiting on you. I haven't seen her this excited about seeing anyone. What do the two of you have up your sleeves today?"

"My daughter and I have a lot to discuss. It's been a long time."

I glanced down at my watch as I followed Marlon. It was almost noon and time for my appointment with my friend and bank manager, Mr. Harrison. Both Suga and I had to be present in order to access the safe deposit box. I had made these arrangements many years ago. In the event of my death, Suga would've been able to secure the contents of the box.

"Hi, Dad," Suga said.

She looked much better from the last time that I saw her. She looked strong and back to her beautiful self. She reminded me so much of her mother. I fought back the thoughts of Teesa as I looked at my daughter. I swallowed hard. My heart skipped a beat when I heard those words. They were like music to my ears. She walked up to me and hugged me. I held her close to me, taking her in. There were so many hugs and kisses that I missed over years that I savored every one she was willing to give me now. She allowed me to hold her in my arms.

"Dad, are you okay?" she asked.

I smiled and said, "Yes, I'm just happy to see you back on your feet," I said.

"Thank God for his healing power. I'm still recovering, but I'm feeling much better. I can't do much with my arm in this cast." She held up her arm that was in a full cast and sling. "I know why you came. You want your money, right?" she asked.

"That's not the only reason why I'm here. I came to check on my baby girl. You were in bad shape when I found you. You had me worried there for a minute."

"I know that's not the only reason why you're here. I know that you're really trying to rebuild our relationship. But don't worry, I'm completely open to it. The past is the past, what matters is that we are together now."

"Thanks for saying that. I really needed to hear that."

"After all that I've been through, I know that life moves at the speed of me. So if I live in the past and continue to hurt those that hurt me, nothing good is going to come from that. Hurt people, hurt people is a true statement. I know first-hand. But now, I can honestly say that I'm truly happy. I have more than I deserve; a man that loves me and a child that I love more than myself."

"I'm sorry, Suga. I'm sorry that I wasn't there for you when you needed me the most. I made many mistakes and it cost me more than I was willing to pay. Just know that here on out, I will do everything I can to make up for the time that I was gone."

"There's no need for that, just be present now. I forgive you and I love you, Dad."

"I love you more than you know."

"I know you do," she said with a smile. "Come on, the money is in the garage."

I followed her out to the garage. I noticed her limp and the painful way in which she walked and went down the two stairs that led down into the garage.

"How's that hip?" I asked.

"It's still in bad shape. With rehab the doctor expects me to recover fully. It's just a setback in my recovery time, but I'll be back to my old self soon," she said.

"Where's your nurse?"

"I gave her the rest of the day off since you were coming. Don't worry I have all the help I need around here."

Suga walked across the garage and pointed at a stack of newspapers. I removed the newspapers and found the exact tub in which I'd placed my money. I opened the top and eyeballed the money, relieved that the amount of money looked accurate.

"All of your money is here. I don't have your other things from the attic. I had Santé sell them, but she hasn't given me any of the money yet," she said.

"Thank you. This is all I have other than the money at the bank. I thought I was coming home to nothing for a minute there." I placed the lid back on the tub. "What were you saying about Santé? I called her to tell her you were home, but I haven't heard from her. Did she go back to New York?" I asked.

"I'm sure she didn't return your call. Don't you know she and Ali planned to rob our store?"

"Wait a minute. What are you talking about? Who told you that? That doesn't sound like Santé. The two of you are like sisters."

"She told me out of her own mouth. I couldn't believe her. She has changed a lot. I guess when you are getting high, you'll do anything."

"Santé is getting high? No, not her."

"Yes. We had this big fight and I haven't heard from her since. We added security to the store to make sure that they didn't try their hand and rob us anyway. She even took all of my money from the things she sold for me."

"I'm going to have to talk to her. I don't understand what's going on with her. She seemed all right when I saw her."

After hearing the news about Santé, something didn't sit right with me. Suga hadn't talked to her and she hadn't returned any of my calls. If I knew anything about a thief, they didn't like anyone taking from them.

"I have a bad feeling about all of this," I said.

"About what? What else can possibly go wrong?" she asked.

"Trust me, never ask that question."

"What's wrong?"

"I think she's in trouble. We have to find her."

"Come on, I don't have anything to say to her."

"I don't care about you being mad at her right now. She's family and I think she's in trouble."

I kneeled down to pick up the tub. Suga opened the garage door so that I could carry it out to the car.

"Meet me in the car. I need you to go with me to the bank and to find your cousin," I said.

Suga didn't answer me, but she moved to my command. I waited for her in the car. I tried to remember the hotel where Santé was staying. Then I remembered it, it was the same hotel where I had the affair with Sable. I had to get to the bank and then to the hotel. I prayed that we would find Santé there safe and sound. My gut said otherwise.

Suga came out to the car and her mood had changed. I knew she was mad about checking on Santé, but her feelings were irrelevant when it came to someone else's safety. For all I knew, she could've went back to New York and cut off communication with us, but I had to be sure.

CHAPTER 25

Suga

Being with my father didn't feel as strange as I thought it would. He was still that cool laid-back person that I remembered. He always made me laugh with his lame jokes when I was little and it still worked. He made a few jokes here and there on our ride to break the tension between us. I didn't understand why he was so concerned about Santé after I told him what she had done. I understood that she was his niece, but I was sure that she wasn't in any kind of trouble.

At the bank, gaining access to my father's safe deposit box was fast. It was clear that he and the bank manager were old acquaintances. I could only imagine what they've done for each other in the past. I didn't hover over his shoulders as he removed the contents of the box. I gave my father privacy as I stood close to the exit. One thing that I did notice was the stacks of cash that he removed. It seemed that he had money stashed everywhere.

SNOOK

After leaving the bank, I thought about how much my life had changed in just a short period of time. I changed as a person. My thoughts and intentions were more focused on others and not myself. I began to live for my family. My desires even changed. I didn't think about the next designer bag, shoes or dress that I could get Marlon to buy me. I didn't care about the material things anymore. That satisfying feeling I would get from stepping into a brand new pair of twelve hundred dollars shoes now came from waking up to my husband and holding my son.

"Are you okay over there? I know that you're upset with me for trying to take you to find Santé, but if you really want to go back home, I'll take you home," my father said.

I thought for a moment. Had this same situation came about a few weeks ago I wouldn't be so much as in the car with my own father. This was just confirmation that I was changing into a better person.

As mad and disappointed in Santé as I was, I knew that I couldn't turn my back on her. I would feel bad if something did happen to her and I didn't at least try to make sure that she was all right. Those feelings took me back to when Kendra was in the hospital after we had our big fight. I turned my back on her and cut her out of my life. Even when she was in the hospital fighting for her life, I didn't come until it was too late to matter. I could've been there for her. I could've been the strength and encouragement she needed to keep fighting, but I wasn't. I didn't want the same thing to happen again.

"No, I'll help you find her. I'm a work in progress and the right thing to do is to make sure she's all right," I said.

"That's my girl," my father said.

He nudged me playfully and I nudged him back.

"I know I've been gone a long time, but I can see a difference in you. When you came to see me in prison for the first time, you were cold. I could see the hurt and pain in your eyes. Now when I look at you I see a warm, loving person. We go through things in life in order to learn from it. The same goes for me," he said.

"Marlon and I have started over. It's best that we move forward in our relationship. It's too much bad for me to revisit. I'm sure he feels the same way."

"Don't blame yourself for all of your marital problems. Women always seem to accept the blame when things go wrong in their relationship. Don't do that. There are two people in a marriage. I'm sure Marlon has made mistakes as well."

"Not as many as I have."

"Is it a competition?"

"No, of course not."

"A sin is still a sin."

"I know that. I'm just saying that it's so much that you or anyone else for that matter don't know about me."

My dad didn't respond to that. I assumed that he didn't want to know all of the evil and selfish things that his precious daughter had done. I quickly changed the subject. It was evident that he didn't want to hear my confessions.

"This is the hotel where she said she was staying," he said. "I'm not sure about the room number so let's ask the front desk."

We stepped out of the car. I took a little longer to get

out. My father assisted me. We walked into the office.

"Hello. My niece Santé White is staying here. I know that you can't tell me what room she's in, but can you let her know that I'm here to see her," he said.

"Did you try calling the room?" the clerk asked.

"Of course, I did. When you connected me there was no answer," he said.

"Let me see," the clerk said.

We waited as she typed something into the computer. Her facial expression quickly changed as she read the computer screen. I knew that something was wrong.

"What? What's wrong?" I asked.

"Let me get my manager," she said.

She rushed off and knocked on the office door. My father and I looked at each other.

"Something is wrong," I said.

My father wore a pained look on his face. The two women whispered in hushed tones and the clerk looked back at us.

"What is the problem?" I asked loudly.

The women ended their conversation and the manager slowly approached us while the clerk remained where she stood.

"There was an incident in the room that Santé White was staying in. The authorities were contacted and she was taken to the hospital. That's about all that I know," the manager said.

"What happened to her?" I asked.

"I'm not sure. She was found in her room unconscious. That's all I know. You will need to contact the hospital or police for more information. Sorry, I can't help you any further," the manager said.

The manager walked away and retreated back into the safety of her office. The clerk appeared scared and didn't dare come back to the front desk. She walked away and disappeared into the back. We were left standing there to figure out what to do next.

On our way back to the car, I immediately began to call the local hospitals to see if they had Santé as a patient. The first hospital I tried had her. Everyone seemed to always end up at VCU Medical Center when they suffered some sort of trauma. I sat in the car as I waited to be transferred to her room. All the while, I thought about what could've happened to her. The best thing that I came up with was that Ali fucked her up for snitching. I motioned for my father, who was still on the phone standing outside of the car, to get in.

"I found her! She's at VCU Medical Center," I told him.

"Good, I'm on the phone with one of my friends from the police department," he said.

I waited as I was connected to her room. Someone finally answered but it wasn't Santé.

"Hello?" a soft voice answered.

"Hi, I'm looking for my cousin Santé White," I said

"This is Ms. White's room. Who is this?" a woman asked.

"I'm her cousin, Suga. We just found out that she was in the hospital," I said.

"We've been trying to contact her family, but wasn't able to make contact with anyone. If you come to the hospital someone will be able to show you to her room."

"Thank you so much. We're on our way."

For the entire ride to the hospital, my father was on the

phone with his friend. My nerves were bad and the feeling of the unknown hunted me. I was still traumatized by all of the things that I'd been through. I prayed that whatever happened to Santé that she was going to be all right. I waited for my father to end his conversation.

"They're saying that she overdosed. She was found by housekeeping," he said.

"Where was Ali?" I asked.

"Nowhere to be found. She was found alone."

"I hope that he didn't do that to her. I told you that she admitted that she was getting high. That was her excuse for trying to rob us."

"What did you find out?"

"Not much. It must be bad if a nurse answered her phone. She didn't even try to put her on the phone."

"Pray."

I dreaded going back to the hospital. I hated hospitals at this point. I found myself in and out recently and it gave me chills just thinking about seeing Santé there. My anxiety was already out of control. All of this was too much to handle. I needed to calm my nerves. Although I didn't want to but I had to take a Xanax in order to deal with the situation at hand. I took out my pill bottle and swallowed it dry .

CHAPTER 26

Marlon

arlon, Jr. and I were lying down for a nap after giving him a bottle. Suga was out with her father and wasn't expected to be back for a couple of hours. The doorbell woke me from my sleep. I rubbed my eyes as I rose from the sofa. I looked over to see if the baby was still asleep, he was. I dragged myself to the front door.

"Who is it?" I asked through the door.

"Detective Wilkes. I need to have a word with you," a voice said from the other side of the door.

I quickly ran over my story that I'd rehearsed over and over for this very moment. I took a deep breath and calmed my nerves. I opened the door.

"How can I help you?" I asked.

Detective Wilkes walked in without being invited. I held the door open longer than needed to get my point across. I closed the door and then stood directly in front of him so that he couldn't advance any further into my home.

"I asked how I could help," I said.

"It seems like just yesterday I was here. Déjà vu is what they call it."

I didn't respond and stood my ground.

"I came here to notify you that De'Angelo Perry was found deceased in his home," Detective Wilkes said.

I took a deep breath and said, "What? Are you telling me that Dee is dead? What happened?"

I slowly let down my guard and began to relax. I tried to appear as distraught as possible. I paced the floor and held my face in my hand to appear shocked at the news.

"Somehow I have a feeling that you knew that already. I mean, you haven't spoken to him have you? When was the last time you spoke with Mr. Perry?"

"We don't talk on the phone every day."

"When was the last time you spoke with him?"

"A few days ago. He seemed fine when I talked to him."

Detective Wilkes gave me a knowing look as if he knew that I wasn't being all the way honest with him. I was well aware of my body language and how he was studying me. I wasn't going to give myself away.

"It's fair to say that you and your wife are losing your friends to such tragic circumstances. Her friend was murdered and now your friend. Wouldn't you say that's a coincidence?"

"So, now you want to pin a murder on me and my wife? How disrespectful of you. That was my friend. We aren't some serial killers going around killing our friends. The real killers are out there somewhere."

"It's my job to investigate these murders. In a lot of cases, victims are killed by those closest to them." He took a brief pause and said, "Where's your wife? You know we needed to speak to her about her friend Lynda Cunningham."

"My wife is out right now. I told you that she didn't have anything to do with that. You tried to convince me that she set me up for that murder and tried to turn me against her. It didn't work. My wife and I are fine. We are honest people making an honest living."

"That's what they all say."

"Are you here to inform me about my best friend's murder or are you here to arrest me. Because one of your jobs is done. I need to contact his family."

Detective Wilkes slapped a small notepad in his hand and began to proceed past me. I blocked him with my body.

"Well, I came here to inform you that Mr. Perry was found dead in his burning home. We received a call for a house fire. To our surprise, his body was discovered inside," Detective Wilkes said.

"Why was the house on fire? Where was his daughter?" I asked.

I held my breath for an answer.

"We found out later that his daughter was with family."

"Thank, God!" I let out a sigh of relief.

"You have even more to thank him for. There were three weapons recovered from the house. One matches the weapon used to kill Ms. Cunningham. We are waiting on ballistics to see if it was the same weapon used. If so, then you won't have to see my face again... Not unless someone else dies."

"Good thing, this is the last time I'll see you."

Detective Wilkes walked towards the door. I followed behind him.

"Oh, one more thing. If Mr. Perry committed those murders, the next question is why?"

I didn't respond. I opened the door for him.

"Thanks for your time. If you hear anything, please let me know," I said.

I just stared at him.

"I'm sure you will," he said.

I watched him walk to his car. He sat in his car for a minute before leaving. My heart was racing. Detective Wilkes was very intimidating. He acted as if he knew that I had something to do with Dee's murder. I knew that if he had real evidence he would've arrested me. I was confident that they would clear us in both situations.

CHAPTER 27

Santé

I was awakened by a nurse who was checking my vitals. The same nurse who talked to me every time she came into my room. Normally, the nurses came in to do their job and leave, but not Nurse Lori. She came in smiling and talking up a storm. She didn't care if I responded to her or not she just kept right on talking. To be honest, she made me feel alive when I felt dead on the inside. My world crumbled at my feet. Waking up each day reminded me just how fucked up my life had become.

"You have a visitor on the way to see you. Do you want to freshen up before she arrives?" Nurse Lori asked.

"How do you know? Who's coming? No one knows I'm here?" I said.

She began to fold back the sheets. I grabbed the sheets and pulled them back over me.

"She said that she was your cousin. Isn't that great?" she asked.

I didn't respond.

"It's always nice to have visitors here. It's no fun sitting here alone is it?" she asked.

"If you say so," I said.

She smiled and tried to fold down the sheets again. I held the sheets tightly.

"If you don't want to get up right now, that's fine. I can bring you a comb and mirror if you like."

"That's all right."

"Suit yourself."

"I just want to rest."

"We have to get some food in you. I have some soup and crackers."

She pulled the tray in front of me. Hospital food wasn't appealing at all. It looked more like broth. There weren't any meat or vegetables in the soup. I turned my nose.

"Come on. Try some soup," she said.

Nurse Lori attempted to give me a spoon of soup, but I turned my head. I was sick to my stomach and didn't have an appetite. My heart was crushed into a million pieces by the one man that I loved; the one man that I was willing to betray my family for.

"You have to eat. We have to get food in to you so that you can get stronger. You're not going to like the other options that we can take to get you to eat. So, why don't you open your mouth and eat this soup? Just a few spoons," she said.

She'd been so tolerant of me. I wasn't the best patient. It was hard for me to accept what Ali did to me. I remembered clearly what happened to me. I remembered it all.

"Okay, just a little bit," I said.

"Good," she said.

She fed me the soup. I ate more than she or I expected. The soup wasn't great but it filled my empty stomach.

"I think a visit from your family will do you some good," she said. "Okay. I'll be back to check on you. Let me know if you need anything."

I turned on the television to distract myself from the negative thoughts that haunted me. My body craved a drug that I wasn't able to readily get my hands on. I needed drug treatment as soon as I was released from the hospital. Without Ali, I didn't want to get high, but my body craved it.

I flipped through a few channels to find something that would catch my attention and keep my mind off of drugs and Ali. I settled on a cartoon that I'd never seen before. Cartoons always made you feel like a child again. It took me to a safe place. I settled on the channel and waited for Suga. I didn't have to wait long before I heard my uncle Linwood's voice.

"What happened?" Linwood asked.

He rushed to my bedside and hugged me. I didn't return the hug, because I didn't have the energy to raise my own arms.

"Are you okay?" Suga asked.

She was standing on my right side. I looked away from her only to be greeted by my uncle's eyes peering down on me. They both seemed to wait patiently for my response. Before I knew it, I was in tears. Suga consoled me, burying my face into her chest. I was surprised, but I accepted her embrace. Suga consoling me made me cry even harder.

"I'm sorry. I'm so sorry," I cried into her.

She rubbed my back like my mother would've, soothing me.

"It's all right. I know you didn't mean to hurt me. I understand that you have a problem. We're going to get through it," she said.

"I never meant to hurt you. I would've never offered you up to Ali. I was so fucked up for that. Please forgive me," I said.

"I've already forgiven you. You need to forgive yourself. We're going to be all right Santé. I love you," she said.

"That's right. We're family and we're going to be here for each other and support one another," Linwood chimed in.

After a few more moments of uncontrollable crying, I pulled it together.

"Now that you're done with all of that crying, we can talk," Suga said jokingly.

I used a tissue to dry my eyes and blow my nose. By now I sounded completely clogged up from all of the crying. I must admit, crying help lift some of the burdens that I carried with me.

"What happened to you?" Linwood asked.

I looked at them both in shame. Suga lifted my hand and held it in hers. For once, I didn't feel that she was judging me. She'd been through her share of tragedies.

"First of all, I'm sorry for what I did… Well, what I planned to do. I really didn't mean to hurt you Suga. I did take all of the money. I know you told me to give you your money, but I was so mad at you. I told Ali that I told you about our plans to rob the store. He gave me some bad shit. He tried to kill me and took all of the money," I said.

"Don't worry about the money. What's important is that you're okay," Suga said.

"Where's Ali?" Linwood asked.

"I guess he's gone back to New York. Don't do anything stupid because he's not worth it. He can have the money. I'm never going back to New York," I said.

"You know what? Why don't you stay with us? I know that you don't have a place here, so why not stay with me?" Suga said.

"I can't impose on you and Marlon like that, especially after what I've done to you. Marlon probably hates me too," I said.

"Nothing happened. The store is fine. Marlon hired security for the store. If Ali thought about trying to rob the store, he was in for a big surprise. We should've had security from the beginning. You're just keeping us on our toes," she said jokingly.

"I'm really surprised by all of this. I never thought that I would see you again. You were pretty mad at me," I said.

"Trust me. I thought the same thing. I was hurt and angry. But after talking to my dad and realizing that we all make mistakes; I found it in my heart to forgive you. Sometimes we hurt the very ones that we love. I live with those thoughts every day," she said.

"Thank you. But now I have to forgive myself. I've done things that are out of my character. I guess we're both a work in progress. We can help each other," I said.

"The blind leading the blind," Linwood said. "The two of you need to get some help. Now, I'm not trying to hurt your feelings or anything. The both of you have been through it. It won't hurt to sit down and talk to one of those head doctors," he said.

Suga and I laughed, turning our heads quickly towards him. "What?" we both said.

"You both need counseling," he said.

Hearing that from my uncle really put things in perspective for me. I needed a lot of things right now. Suga's invitation to stay with her didn't really sit right with me. I knew that she was trying to change for the better. Change took time and trust was something that she didn't extend often. With my track record, I knew that she didn't fully trust me right now. I didn't want to come between her and her husband in any way. I didn't have anywhere to stay, so I had to take her up on her offer. I was going to stay with her until I was able to get on my feet. I needed to be on my own, but I knew that I had to get help with my addiction first.

"I have to get going. Marlon is waiting on me. I'll be back tomorrow to check on you. Be strong cousin," she said.

"I'll try," I said.

"You're strong. You can beat this," Linwood said.

He also left me with a big hug and kiss. I watched the two of them leave. I wanted to scream out, "Please don't leave me here alone!"

Just as Suga and Linwood were leaving, the doctor walked in. I prayed that neither one would ask any questions or turn back around to see what the doctor had to say. Suga looked back at me with concern. I forced a smile assuring her that all was well.

"Hello, Ms. White. I'm Dr. Holden. How are you feeling?" he asked.

Dr. Holden looked to be in his fifties, short and round. He wore a bald head and glasses. As he spoke to me he didn't make much eye contact.

"I haven't been feeling well. I've been nauseated," I said.

"That's to be expected. You came close to dying. We received the results back from the lab. You took heroin and Fentanyl. That's a deadly combination of drugs. You're lucky to be alive," Dr. Holden said.

"Wow, he really tried to kill me. I knew something didn't look right. He said it was his special blend," I said.

"It was a special blend that could've killed you. Good thing someone called for help. You arrived here just in time," he said.

"Do you have any questions?" he asked.

"When can I go home?" I asked.

"Possibly in a few days or so. We still have to manage your progress and see where we should go from here. You're doing great. Stay strong," he said.

"Thanks, doctor," I said.

I was alone, again. I hated being alone. Left with my thoughts, I laid in the bed and came up with a plan to beat my addiction and better myself. I was going to take Suga up on her offer and show her that I am strong. I wanted to make her proud of me again. Suga was important to me and I didn't want to let her down. After all that had happened, I realized at the end of the day family was the only ones that would be there. Ali was my world and he was nowhere to be found. I was grateful for my family.

CHAPTER 28

Suga

I called Marlon to let him know that we were about to pull up at the house. I was emotionally drained after seeing Santé. I had to fight against the old me and the new me. The old me probably would've whooped her ass on sight. I had to tap into my sensitive side; change wasn't easy. I had to think before I spoke or acted.

When we pulled into the driveway, I expected to see Marlon waiting at the door. He wasn't there as expected. I sat and waited a moment to see if he was going to come out. My anxiety kicked in as I thought back to when Dee ambushed me right in my driveway.

"What's the matter?" my dad asked.

"I thought Marlon was going to be at the door," I said.

"I can walk you to the door. Do you want me to?" he asked.

"Yes, please."

We both got out of the car. My father quickly rushed to

my side of the car and put his arms around me. He walked me to the door. Just as I was about to ring the bell, Marlon opened the door.

"Sorry. I was laying Junior down," Marlon said.

"That's all right," I said.

I was relieved to see him. My father gave me a hug and left. My hip was starting to ache from all of the walking I was doing. I needed to rest. I laid down on the sofa and propped my arm on a pillow. Marlon sat at my feet on the sofa and gently rubbed my legs.

"How did Junior do today? He didn't act up too bad, did he?" I asked.

"No, he ate and slept. Oh, yeah and pooped all over me," he said.

"What? He got you too?"

We both laughed.

"We have to talk."

The mood quickly changed. For the first time, I noticed the look on his face. He was worried about something.

"What's wrong?" I asked.

"Do you remember those detectives that came here after your friend's death?" he asked.

"Yes."

"One of them just paid us a visit."

"For what? We didn't have anything to do with her murder. At first, I thought you had something to with it, but now I know that you didn't. This is my fault. I called the detectives."

"I know what you did. I didn't tell you that they were looking for you the same day that you went missing. They told me that you tried to set me up for the double murder."

"I'm sorry. I was scared. After you made me do that to you… You know what you did to me in the hospital. I didn't trust you after that."

"I'm sorry about that. I hope that you can forgive me for that. That wasn't me at all."

"I know and I already forgave you."

"But I know who killed them," he said.

"You do? Who did it?" I asked.

"Dee killed them both. He was supposed to convince her to leave town and pay her off. I couldn't be with you knowing that L.C. could have you anytime she wanted. I couldn't face the humiliation with her still in this city. I needed her gone. Instead, he killed them and took the money. He tried to set me up."

"When does it end? That monster did so much damage."

"They found Dee's body. They also found the weapon used in L.C.'s murder. Our names are going to be cleared on that. Now they're harassing me about Dee's murder."

"He's dead. Are you sure? But…" I started to say.

"Don't ask me any questions about that," he said.

I knew that Marlon and my father somehow rescued me and handled the situation. But I wasn't sure exactly what went down.

"Baby, tell me everything is going to be all right. I have to hear that," I said.

"Everything is going to be all right. Trust me," he said.

"I can't take anything else happening. Santé is in the hospital right now from taking some bad drugs that Ali gave her. He tried to kill her."

"Is she all right?"

"Yes. I told her that she can stay with us until she gets back on her feet. Is that all right with you?"

I prayed that he would agree. I really wanted to help her. In a way, I was helping myself too.

"Of course. She's family. Anything she needs we got her," he said.

"Thank you, baby."

I looked around my home. It was full of things that I felt I needed to define me and my relationship with Marlon. I had it all. The best of the best. Yet, I felt less than most of the time. I would buy even more things to cover up my feelings. I was trying to get comfortable being naked for a change. I hadn't made any new purchases since I'd been home from the hospital. There was one thing that weighed on me; that was coming clean about Dee. When I tried to bring it up, Marlon would shut me down. He'd rather pick up the pieces and move on. That was good for him, but not for me. I really needed to get it off my chest.

"Do you want me to run you a hot bath so that you can relax your muscles?" he asked.

"Sure. I'm hurting all over."

He placed my legs gently on the sofa as he got up. He walked over to me and kissed me.

"Marlon, I really have something that I need to tell you."

"I told you, no more confessions. They're not needed."

"I know what you said. But I really need to tell you something. I don't know how you're going to feel about me after this, but I have to get this off my chest. This is the only way that we can truly move forward."

Marlon took a deep breath and stepped away from me. He looked down at me and shook his head.

"I already know about you and Dee. He made it a point to tell me right before he died."

Marlon turned to walk away.

"Wait a minute? You knew and didn't say anything?" I asked.

"I told you that I didn't want to talk about this. Are we moving forward or what?" he asked.

"Yes. But don't you think you should hear my side of the story?"

"No, I don't need to hear it. I know why you did it. We both made mistakes and we're still here. That's the end of it."

"I'm sorry, Marlon."

"I'm sorry, too."

The weight lifted off my chest. I could finally breathe. Sleeping with Dee was the ultimate betrayal and now I was free of it. I immediately began to cry. Marlon rushed over to me and held me in his arms as I cried.

"We're good, baby. No more worries," he said.

"I don't deserve your forgiveness, yet you're still here. You didn't have to be here after finding that out. I knew that you truly loved me, but I know it with conviction."

"We're going to be all right. Trust me. The love that we have for one another is unbreakable. We've made all the mistakes, now we have to learn from them."

"Oh, I've learned. I've had one too many brushes with death. My life has changed for the better. God blessed me with you and Marlon, Jr."

"God has blessed us with each other."

I headed upstairs with Marlon's help. He ran me a hot bath as I waited for him. I walked into the nursery to check on Marlon Jr. He was asleep. I rubbed his back gently, careful not to wake him.

"Mommy loves you, baby," I whispered.

"Your bath is ready!" Marlon called out.

I turned to walk away. Standing in the door, I thought I saw Dee. Just as he was the night of my party. I blinked and he disappeared. I breathed heavily. I looked back at my son and he was still asleep. I looked back at the door and no one was there.

I suddenly became nauseous. I grabbed my mouth and ran to the bathroom. I fell to the floor and began to vomit into the toilet.

"Are you okay?" Marlon asked rushing into the bathroom behind me.

"I'm okay. I just felt sick all of a sudden," I said.

"You're sweating. Are you sure you're okay?" he asked.

"I'm okay. I think I overdid it today. I just want to get in the bath and in the bed."

"Come on. Let me help you," he said.

Marlon helped me into the tub. He wrapped my cast so that it wouldn't get wet. I was surprised that he lit my candles that I had placed around the tub.

"Thank you," I said.

"You're welcome. If you need anything else, just let me know. I'll be right here in the bedroom," he said.

"Okay."

SNOOK

I lifted the bath sponge out of the water. I held it over my face and body and allowed the warm soapy water to pour down over my body. It felt so good. I sat back and relaxed. I thought about how thankful I was for everything that I had. I was thankful for life and health. I knew that things could've turned out worse.

CHAPTER 29

Linwood

ona and I stood outside of our new home health care business. We watched as the signage was being installed. I was looking to invest my money in a business and she was looking into going into business for herself. It was the perfect situation for us. We were able to find a great establishment with a prime location for employees and clients. I wasn't knowledgeable in health care, I left that to Mona since she had fifteen years of nursing experience. I was experienced in business and making money.

"We did it!" Mona said.

"Yes, we did. You did a great job picking this location."

"I think we made the right decision to buy this franchise instead of starting our own. It would've been too much with me now expecting."

She rubbed her baby bump and smiled.

"I don't want my baby working too hard. Now that the

hard work is over, I want you to relax. You have a business partner and an office manager, let them do their jobs," I said.

"There's still a lot of work to be done. You don't just turn your business over to others. I'm going to be hands on. I know you wouldn't want nothing more than to have me at home, barefoot and pregnant."

"What's wrong with that?"

"You're such an ass."

In a small matter of time, I was able to rebuild. This time, I was running a legitimate business. Mona was a great woman and I loved her. It took some time for me to trust again, but she slowly knocked down the armor I built around my heart. She was expecting our first child and I put a ring on it as the young folks say. Life had a funny way of breaking me down and then bringing me back from the ashes better than before.

Suga and I were able to build a relationship. I apologized to her for my mistakes and she accepted my apology. After seeing the lengths that Marlon went to for Suga, I had no doubt about him. I couldn't ask for a better man to love and care for my daughter. I was blessed with a grandson that I couldn't wait to get out in the yard with to teach him to play football.

As for Kyle's grimy ass, as much as I wanted to fuck him up for lying and stealing from me, I didn't want to go back to prison. His bitch ass would've had me locked back up. It wasn't until one morning when Mona brought in the newspaper, I read a story about a well-known attorney found guilty of attempted murder of his now ex-wife's lover. I knew that Kyle was going to get what was coming to him, but I didn't see it coming so soon.

Marlon

It was Marlon Jr.'s first birthday. We'd planned an all-out birthday bash at our home with family and close friends. We were having characters, face painting, a moon bounce and even a small petting zoo. We spared no expense for entertaining the little ones at his first birthday party. I was up all night preparing for the day.

"Daddy! Daddy! Get up!" Marlon Jr. repeated as Suga coached him on what to say.

"Tell him to get up," she whispered.

I pretended that I was still asleep.

"Get up!" he said.

I rolled over and grabbed him, tickling him.

"Why are you jumping on my bed little monster? I'm going to get you!" I said.

Marlon Junior fell over in laughter.

SNOOK

Suga joined us on the bed as she jumped to his defense, tickling me too.

"Oh, you want some too," I said.

I immediately stopped tickling my son and went after her. She tried to resist me, but couldn't. All three of us laughed and tickled each other.

"It's almost noon. It's time to get ready for the birthday party. The animals are already here and ruining the yard," Suga said.

"Who's the birthday boy? How old are you going to be today?" I asked.

Marlon Junior held up one finger and said, "One."

"Yes! That's right. You're one year old today!"

He began to jump on the bed again.

"I'm getting up," I said.

"We'll let you get ready. Meet us downstairs. We need help with the decorations and moving some things around. Hurry up, baby!" she said.

"I'll be down."

"Santé is on her way over with the cake. I hope she doesn't drive like a maniac and ruin it."

"I love you, woman."

"I love you too. But you're not getting out of helping with this party."

"I wasn't trying to get out of it. I just wanted to tell you that I love you."

"I know you love me."

I watched Suga and Marlon Jr. leave the bedroom hand in hand. Suga was an awesome mother. I loved how she loved our son. After everything that we've been through we still managed to keep our marriage intact. We had our good days and our bad days, but we made it through. Thanks to marriage counseling with our pastor, we were able to work through all of our issues and our hurt.

After finding out the reason that Suga slept with Dee, I was able to sort through those feelings better. I was numb to it at first. I suspected that something was going on when he showed up at the hospital with a gag gift insinuating that he was the father of Marlon, Jr. At the time, I took my anger out on Suga. That was something that I begged her forgiveness for. My actions that day were completely out of character.

I found that I had to deal with the fact that I wasn't the only man that Suga had been with. I prided my relationship with her on that fact. Even though she hit me way below the belt, I couldn't blame her for trying to get back at me for sleeping with Kendra. She thought that I had a baby with her best friend. Dee's manipulation helped convince her that what she was doing would even the score. I would be lying if I didn't say that it still bothered me at times. I knew that I had to accept that it happened and move on. The way that I dealt with it was knowing that Dee was gone and could never hurt my family again.

Ironically, we became Destiny's guardians. We were her godparents. Kendra and Dee made sure that they let their families know what their wishes were and had it placed in their will. At first, I didn't feel right having her around after all that happened. Then I thought about it, it was the right thing to do. Destiny was innocent in all of this. We were her godparents before our friendships fell apart. We had to uphold our responsibility. Suga was elated to have Destiny in our family.

Watching Suga grow from her painful past was like watching a rose grow from concrete, it was a miracle. She was stronger than I ever thought she could be. Anyone would've crumbled and given up after being dealt one bad hand after another. Her smile was wider and brighter. Her smile was no longer made from the material things that I gave her to make her happy like in the past. She smiled when she awoke in the morning, she smiles when she sees me each day, she smiles when she looks at our son. I know that she is truly happy and for the right reasons.

I have no regrets for wanting to work on our marriage. Even though at times it seemed dark and impossible, I always knew that there was light at the end of the tunnel.

I truly had it all. I had a beautiful wife, a handsome son, and a family that loved and supported each other, no matter what. I'd come to learn that nothing comes without flaws.

CHAPTER 31

Suga

We watched as Destiny and Marlon Jr. played together in the moon bouncer. They'd grown so close since she moved in. It took some adjustment for us all. I saw a lot of me in her. I knew what it was like to be without parents and having to live with someone else. My experiences prepared me for raising her.

Santé had some of the children lined up for face painting. She was dressed as a clown. Some of the children didn't want to come near her while others fought to the front of the line to have their faces painted. We were so proud of her for going to a treatment program. After the ordeal with Ali and her drug addiction, she was able to overcome them both. She volunteered her time helping women with an addiction. She worked full-time and was now in her own apartment. We were closer than ever and continued to support each other.

SNOOK

My father was back on his feet. He and Mona were expecting their first child together. At first, I didn't know how to feel about the news that he was having another child. Mona was younger than my father. I anticipated that she would eventually want children. Once I was over the initial shock, I accepted the fact that I was going to be a big sister even though there was going to be a huge age gap.

Uncle Redd was still like a father to me. He didn't fall back when my father came back, he remained the same. Although my father was around, he still held a special place in my heart like a father. He didn't miss a moment in my life or my son's. He and Allyssa were doing well. He was planning his retirement in a few months and planned to travel. He deserved it. After all he'd done for me and others, he deserved to relax and enjoy his life.

Marlon and I were having the time of our lives. We were in a space where we both could truly be who we were. We loved each other unconditionally. My love wasn't based on what he did for me and how much materialistic things I possessed. I knew I would love him even if we were broke with only two nickels to rub together.

Our names were cleared in the murders of L.C. and her girlfriend. The police matched the gun found in Dee's home with the gun used in their murders. Dee's murder went unsolved. Business is good and life is good. I'm still a work in progress and I'm progressing. I still love money and nice things, but learned that I can't cover myself with those things. It's okay to be naked. Being myself is okay. The good, the bad and the ugly.

One thing that I learned from all of this is that all things done in the dark, soon comes to light. Although my life wasn't perfect, it's much better than it had been months ago. Karma is real; whatever you put out in the universe, you will get in return. When karma kissed me, it was one hell of a kiss. I'm Suga and I have been kissed by karma in more ways than one.

To learn more about Snook
and her novels, visit

www.snooknovels.com